THE HOUSE ON ROUND HILL ROAD

DEBORAH LIVESEY

To order additional copies of this book, contact:
Bookwhip
1-855-339-3589
https://www.bookwhip.com

ONE

A Death in the Family

Deirdre sat at her desk poring over the list of roses that would be available from their supplier in February. The nursery she and her husband, Jeremy, owned had not had as much success selling roses the previous season as she had expected and, certainly, hoped. She was intent on improving last year's performance. Absorbed in the task at hand, she absentmindedly twirled a lock of her blonde hair with her fingers. At this point, her most important job was deciding which tried-and-true and which colorful, new varieties of roses would move in the marketplace. Her imagination was captured by the splashes of color and the wafts of scents you can only get in early summer.

The ringing phone interrupted her summer fantasies. It was unusual to get a call so early in the morning, just after breakfast. Most people were not yet ready to start the day with outdoor activities, especially at this time of the year. Work in the garden had slowed to a trickle. She certainly did not expect to hear from anyone, either known or unknown. Wondering who the early bird might be, she answered.

"Deirdre?" Emily's voice at the other end of the line was quaking.

"Em, what's wrong? You sound like you've just seen a ghost!"

Emily burst out crying, not something Deirdre ever expected from her older sister. Emily always seemed to be the well-adjusted daughter in the Lincoln family. She managed to get her words out through what sounded like a torrent of tears. "It's Mother. She had a coronary."

Deirdre paused long enough to find the right words. "Is she going to be okay?"

The answer came quickly, accompanied by uninterrupted sobbing. "She didn't make it."

Deirdre paused again. This time there were no right words. *She's too young, younger than Daddy was when he died.* She choked back tears, surprised at the hollow feeling she suddenly had within. She was at a loss about how she should continue. "Em, talk to me."

"Oh, Deirdre. It happened. So unexpectedly."

With a difficulty she didn't quite understand, Deirdre pulled herself together. She realized that, for some strange reason, Emily was in better shape than she was. Probably because Emily had had an hour longer to digest the news. Deirdre was certain their younger sisters had no knowledge of what had happened but asked anyway. "Have you called Caroline and Penelope yet? I'll do that if you'd like. Or maybe you'd prefer to call Caroline."

Without hesitation, Emily answered, "I'll call Caroline. You should be the one to call Penelope."

Deirdre confirmed that she would make the call as soon as she hung up. Then she'd make her plane reservation. "I'll be on the first flight I can get. I'll call back, probably within an hour or two, with the flight information. Meanwhile, start a list of stuff for me to do." With that, Deirdre ended the conversation. Her next thought had been to call Jeremy into the office and tell him. Instead, she decided that she really needed to call Penelope without delay. Assuring herself that she was composed, she lifted the receiver from its cradle and dialed Penelope. As the phone rang and rang, she remembered that Tuesdays were Penelope's errand day. The orchestra did not rehearse on Tuesdays, so that left Penelope time to tackle the mundane chores of daily life. Penelope always had a backlog of things to be done. Deirdre was about to hang up when a breathless Penelope answered.

She offered an explanation for her breathlessness. "I was just unlocking the door when I heard the phone ringing. I had to juggle the keys, groceries, and OddJob before I could answer." OddJob was her bruiser of a cat, always trying to find a way outside, if not by guile, then by brute force. "Hey, what's the call in the middle of the day for?"

"I don't know how to make this any easier – for either of us. Oh, baby, there is no easy way to say this. Penelope, Mother died this morning."

Silence. Neither one of them was ready to fill the gap Deirdre's words had created. Finally, drawing a deep breath, Penelope said, "I was just there last weekend. She was fine. When I left, we had had a minor disagreement. Deirdre, how can I ever forget that she and I were at odds when she died?" After another pause, she went on. "Are you coming? I hope so. I need your company."

Deirdre responded with immediacy, "Jeremy has to be told. Then I'm going to call the airline and get the first flight to Boston I can. I'll call Emily back with my arrival time. She's real shook up. She could use some sisterly company too."

"I ought to be able to get ten days off. I'll go to North Linton tonight. We'll have to start going through the house, getting rid of our junk and probably a lot of Mother's too. We can talk about all this later," Penelope said.

Deirdre wrapped up the call. "I love you, sweetie. I'll see you faster than you can say East Coast. Bye for now." Informing Jeremy was the next order of business. She pushed the button that served to activate their primitive paging system. As she waited for him, she worked on a viable scenario to present to Jeremy before they started talking. Deirdre and Jeremy had been planning to fly east in November to spend Thanksgiving with the family. Instead, she would fly there now, alone, to attend her mother's funeral. It was appropriate that she and her sisters would be together, once again, to shore each other up. What now seemed the likeliest plan was that she would spend the time until Thanksgiving in the house on Round Hill Road. She would do her part in preparing the house for sale, not an inconsiderable effort. After Jeremy joined her in North Linton for a somewhat subdued holiday, they would drive back across the country in a rental truck, bringing home what she deemed worthy of rescue from the past. As these thoughts congealed, she formulated the words that she wanted to use when talking with her husband.

Deirdre didn't have to wait long before Jeremy showed up at the office door. She allowed herself an unexpected show of emotions, throwing herself into his arms and clinging tightly as she told him about Emily's phone call. She was aware that the loss of a family member was a new experience for him. Never having experienced a family loss himself, he seemed to be taken aback by Deirdre's behavior. She was as surprised at her reaction to the news as Jeremy was. They had had enough conversations about Deirdre's rocky relationship with her mother to think that this would pass without much emotion.

When Deirdre relaxed her grip, Jeremy sat down at his desk. The room held two simple desks, one or the other of which was always overflowing with papers and, oftentimes, plants. It was highly unusual for both Deirdre and Jeremy to be in the tiny office at the same time. Whoever was not in the office was usually in the greenhouse. More often than not, they were both in the greenhouse.

Deirdre gave Jeremy a long look. Then she gave him her thoughts about the foreseeable future. Jeremy cocked his head and then agreed with her. He would stay behind, and she would spend two months with her family. "Are you going to be okay all alone in that big house? I mean, I've never heard you express a desire to return there." Jeremy's voice was full of concern.

Deirdre responded without delay, happy that he understood the differing forces at work on her. "Emily will come over most days. Don't know about Caroline, but I'm sure that Penelope will spend extra time in North Linton."

After further discussion of the day's events, Deirdre turned to arranging an immediate flight to Boston. Jeremy stayed with her while she made the reservations. To her surprise, a number of seats were still available. Getting there wasn't going to be a problem. In the old days, airlines used to offer bereavement discounts, with the express intention of helping relieve unexpected expenses. Not anymore.

After making her plane reservation, Deirdre called Emily back to let her know when she would arrive, but all she got was an answering machine. That was understandable, given the turmoil Emily's household was sure to be in. Deirdre left a brief message, just stating the bare bones and nothing else. After that, and after working to leave what she had been doing before the fateful call in reasonable shape, it was her intention to rush home and pack. She was still experiencing the shock of the past few hours. She was, in addition, reviewing the past twenty-plus years.

❦

Since moving to the West Coast fifteen years earlier, Deirdre had returned to New England only three times – twice for family visits and the last time for her father's funeral. This time, it would be for her mother's funeral. While she had loved her father immeasurably, she had had a hard time even thinking of spending time with her mother. It was ironic that her mother was now responsible, however indirectly, for this trip home.

Her father had died shortly before his retirement, leaving her mother a fairly young widow. Her mother had quickly slipped into the role of a crusty dowager, a role she'd seemingly been rehearsing for years. She was a true lily of the field – she toiled not; neither did she spin, cook, clean, or do anything else that didn't appeal to her. Deirdre had often wondered how she and her sisters had survived until Emily had assumed the role of head cook at the age of sixteen. Somewhere along the line it had become clear to Deirdre what an enormous amount of work their father had done in raising them and keeping the household running smoothly all those years. She had been too young to notice that he had prematurely aged. The years of added responsibility had softened his marvelous, sharp features and made that thick mop of brown hair turn white.

The last time the four sisters had been together had been for their father's funeral. While this was another somber occasion, Deirdre was looking forward to seeing all her sisters together at the same time. It was likely that the opportunities to enjoy their company would continue to be less and less frequent. So much had happened in their lives in the intervening years. While each was fundamentally the same person she had always been, all of them had been shaped by new and different experiences. When Deirdre had moved West, Caroline had just entered law school, Penelope had barely begun college, and Emily had not yet had any of her three children.

Of the four of them, Deirdre had been the most affected by her father's death. This time, Emily would feel the loss the most acutely. Emily had married her childhood sweetheart and settled in the same town where they had all grown up. She usually saw their mother once or twice a week, in large part because their mother enjoyed her grandchildren so much. In contrast to Emily, each of the others had chosen not to return to North Linton after college. None of them was close to their mother. Deirdre had first lived in Rhode Island and then moved to Washington State with the intention of putting three thousand miles between her mother and herself. After graduating from college, Caroline had gone to law school and then moved to Washington, DC, and worked for various progressive policy organizations. There, she had fallen in love with a like-minded colleague. Amazingly enough to her, the feeling had been mutual. They were married in a private ceremony after a whirlwind courtship. Penelope had been the only family member present.

Following the tradition of her two older sisters, Penelope had gone off on her own when she too graduated from college. She'd moved to New York City to pursue her music career there. After a few years of pickup jobs and lots of waitressing, she had finally landed a position as a flautist with an orchestra in Hartford, Connecticut.

Each of the three younger sisters had chosen a career involving one of the interests their father had been passionate about – gardening, progressive politics, and classical music. Only Emily had been influenced by their mother and had followed the more traditional path. She had had children and decided to stay home with them. Currently, she was doing freelance writing at home, producing a weekly column of general commentary that ran in the local newspaper. Her columns were well received by both the editorial staff and the readers in general.

⁓ ❧ ⁓

Pulled back from her thoughts about family, Deirdre knew she had little time to waste. She had to get back home and do as much preparation for the next two months as she possibly could. The term *home* caused her to reevaluate which place she was referring to. That word had so many different meanings. It seemed that she was about to go from one *home* to another. Maybe that would be something she could contemplate on the flight between her two *homes*. The nursery would do fine without her, which both relieved and disappointed her. She was relieved but left with that lingering feeling that maybe she was not as indispensable as she liked to think she was. There were a few things she absolutely had to do before she left, but the nursery wouldn't fall apart without her.

After accomplishing the few tasks that needed to be done that afternoon, Deirdre collected Jeremy, and they headed home. Recently, they had devised a system for meeting the most pressing needs of every day. One would stay to close the nursery while the other returned home to cook dinner. Considering what had happened that day, their manager sent them home together. They only had a short drive since they lived close to the nursery. Once home, Jeremy took two prepared dinners, bought for just such a hurried occasion, out of the freezer and popped them in the oven. Deirdre had, meanwhile, slumped into a nearby chair. The dinners didn't take long to heat. Deirdre and Jeremy ate them in relative silence.

After dinner was over, Deirdre went upstairs to get packed for her long absence. Every flannel and wool item of clothing she owned went into the suitcase. After a short time, Jeremy joined her. He let her be the one to break the silence.

Finally, she did. "I hope nothing unforeseen happens while I'm gone," she said with concern. "I have no doubt you'll handle anything that comes up with no problem. And you'll always have Amy there to help. We were smart to hire her. Anyway, I'm almost finished packing. Let's get to bed early. I've got a long day ahead of me."

THE FLIGHT EAST

As the plane sped down the runway, Deirdre settled back into her seat and contemplated the upcoming days. It was almost a relief to be underway. Deirdre had never been a good traveler. She worried about every detail of every trip. She had once almost missed a flight to London because Europe ends daylight savings time on a different date than the United States does. The near miss had only added to her arsenal of worries. The abrupt nature of this journey had given Deirdre no time to fret. It was still just as well, though, that she was making this trip alone. She certainly was no treat to travel with.

The phone call from her sister, Emily, had come as a complete shock. Deirdre planned to spend the next two months organizing the contents of the house she had grown up in and, along with her sisters, would divide and disperse everything, large and small, from the biggest piece of furniture to the smallest kitchen utensil. Deirdre was just beginning to envision the work of the days ahead when she was jolted out of her thoughts by the flight attendant, coming by with the breakfast cart.

The flight attendant was a woman, but in no other way did she fit the image of a stewardess that had been current when Deirdre was growing up. Instead, this woman was in her late thirties and, while not fat, was certainly ample. She was even wearing slacks! When Deirdre was eleven, after she had ripped through all the Nancy Drew books, she had read a short series about an airline stewardess – what was her name? – where the stewardesses all had to be unmarried, attractive, and size 8. She was grateful that the women's movement had come along to eliminate those restrictions.

At this juncture, there was no point in absorbing herself in the reason for the trip and what she hoped to accomplish while there. Interruptions would be relentless. She hated airline meals but knew the aisles would now be blocked throughout the flight by the cumbersome carts, with attendants dispensing beverages and substandard food. Her thoughts about the present could wait.

Instead, she decided to think about the word *home*. Perhaps because she was closest to the *home* she was living in now, with Jeremy, she should start there. Granted, they both spent most of their time at the nursery, but their house was their *home*. Actually, the house and the nursery were both *home*. It was the vicinity where they belonged. Maybe that was the key. *Belonged.* In her college years, she had lived in many different dorms, but throughout the entire time she had *belonged* at that college. She'd never thought of that place as *home*, but she guessed it had been.

She had learned different things in each of her various *homes*. As a child, her early classroom was her first *home* – the house on Round Hill Road. There, one of her first lessons was about the cycle of the seasons – summer with its flowers, birds, and those dastardly foes: mosquitoes; winter with the falling snowflakes, the big piles of snow at the sides of the roads, the gleaming ice to skate on and the frigid cold that made her nostrils stick together; and the transitional seasons that really only served to remind her that something big was in the works, right around the corner. Throughout it all, there were those wonderful puffy, white clouds. There was, obviously, so much more, but that was the foundation of her early life and, she suspected, of the early lives of most children.

At that point, the pilot came on the intercom to tell the passengers they were beginning to fly over the mountains. In her mind, Deirdre could see the first signs of the winter that was still a few months away for the lowland dwellers. From her past experience, she knew it could snow as early as Labor Day in the mountains. She had gone to college in California. Crossing the country, both by land and air, was nothing new to her. At one time or another, she had visited most parts of the country. In the course of her college years, she had gone home with classmates during school breaks; she'd camped out at other times; and, when she could really afford the extravagance, had stayed in simple motels on her way to and from school. The country's variety of regional climates was quite familiar to her.

Every September, Deirdre had driven to college. The first year, she had gone west with her parents, leaving home in mid-August and taking a slow, circuitous route to reach the opposite coast. They had gone to places she had only read and dreamed about. South Dakota, with its gently rolling topography and lush green vegetation, had captivated her. She had only rosy recollections of that state, highlighted by great memories of Mount Rushmore and the Black Hills. Then they'd moved on to Wyoming, another state with unforgettable scenery. The magnificence of the Grand Tetons still took her breath away. She could also never forget the wondrous vision of Devil's Tower. She had never seen anything like it, with its marked striations. Whether anyone had ever reached the top still baffled her. If so, how? And why? It was only then that she'd started to have a glimmer of appreciation for the widely varying geology of this country. The next stop on their extended journey had been the Grand Canyon. It was an extreme example of America's geological wonders. She still was in awe of its beauty and speechless to describe it. While she had been struck by its superlatives, she had most relished the opportunity to stand at the junction of four states at once. Mundane, but true.

After that unmatchable experience, it had been on to California and college. In those days, college started in September, not August. Otherwise, the trip would not have been possible.

The whole trip had been her mother's idea. Deirdre had been anxious to get to California and had wanted to hurry. But her mother's plans had prevailed – as they always had. Deirdre had to admit that, at least this time, her mother's idea had been a good one. They had driven at a leisurely pace through the vast midsection of the country.

Deirdre had learned about and developed an affection for that part of America. What she most remembered was that the landscape was green as far as the eye could see. At that time of year, the cornfields were topped by gold. The corn, mature with tassels adding an additional color to break up the green monotony, was better than any corn she had ever eaten before. In all the subsequent years, the prospect of eating mouth-watering corn-on-the-cob on the cross-country drive to college helped to mitigate any sadness that went along with the end of summer. The beginning of a new school year, with its unknown adventures and challenges, held its own attractions. One never knew what was in store. Every new year was a fresh start.

On that trip, she had learned that, in the Midwest, the roads are flat and straight. They go on for miles. All of a sudden, one can find oneself going ninety miles per hour on the interstate without a second thought. There are also innumerable restaurants along the highway. It was easy to find a place to stop and get a good, cheap meal. Deirdre thought back fondly to the hearty pancake breakfasts with big slabs of bacon on the side. After one of those breakfasts, she had seen a working beehive behind glass in a wall of the restaurant. Pancakes from wheat, bacon from pigs, honey from bees. The whole breakfast had been one of those marvelous lessons of seeing firsthand where food actually comes from. The only thing that was missing was maple syrup, and only a New Englander would miss that.

After her second year of college, Deirdre and her college roommate, Betty, had headed off to Colorado and spent the summer living and working in a tony resort town in the mountains. Her most enduring memory of that summer – and there were many – was the rainbow she saw while riding her bike down the main street. The rainbow peeked out from behind the mountains to the east, arched over the town, and disappeared behind the mountains to the west. Other memories included nights spent in the mountains looking up at the stars, poking around in deserted ghost towns, and just wading in rushing streams. She had been a bread chef at a big restaurant in town. That learning experience had, in itself, made the summer worthwhile. It had been a summer of learning – about how to bake bread; about herself; about living as a grown-up. The latter was a good lesson for what Deirdre would face in only two years' time. At the end of that summer in Colorado, she and Betty had driven back to college, visiting different sites that she had not seen before and broadening her knowledge of America. The next summer had been spent living at home and working in town – a last reminder of life in the bosom of family, such as it was.

The pilot broke in to announce that the plane was approaching turbulence and seatbelts should be fastened. Deirdre looked out the window to see what lay below. The plane was now over the flat Midwest. Flying over it presented a very different picture from driving through it. The country was like a big brown and green checkerboard from this height. Next would come the rust belt – Indiana, Michigan and Ohio. No rust that she could see. Only dilapidated factories. Many. Then came Pennsylvania with its rolling hills. At least the part she knew and loved. Then her beloved New England. In contrast to the Midwest, the New England landscape would just now be beginning to don its autumn mantle of colors. While the colors were not yet visible from the air, in another week to ten days the countryside would be aflame with crimson, orange, and gold. She suspected that Thomas Wolfe was correct and that you can't go home again. Not that she would want to relive those days, but she was glad to know that Wolfe's prescient observations did not apply to the foliage. In the days ahead, while clearing out her mother's house and getting it prepared for sale, she knew that she would be spending a lot of time there alone, among the old familiar trees dressed up in their autumn finery. She knew that, as she spent time at the house, she would be surrounded by the old stalwarts. There would be issues of the past that she needed to address, ghosts she wanted to confront.

The rest of the flight went by more quickly than she had anticipated. Soon they were circling over the airport in Boston. The landing at Logan was as nerve-wracking as usual. Deirdre had never gotten used to the fact that the runway there was only a scant distance from the water.

After the long flight, Deirdre mentally prepared herself for the next part of the family saga. There would be good times and bad times, but you couldn't have one without the other. Wasn't there a song that said that?

ARRIVAL AT THE AIRPORT

As soon as the plane landed in Boston, Deirdre unbuckled her seat belt, a small gesture of defiance to the airline. The flight attendant had given the usual spiel about keeping the seat belts buckled until the plane was at the gate. Why Deirdre needed to comply was beyond her comprehension. The plane was on the ground; the riskiest part of the flight was already over. When the plane finally did reach the gate, Deirdre was on her feet before anyone else could plant him or herself by the overhead bin above her seat. She got out her carry-on bags and, under her breath, uttered silent thanks that she was at the front of what she jokingly referred to as steerage. At least she would be among those who were earliest off the plane.

Deirdre was anxious to get to baggage claim and find out who was there to meet her. With any luck, it would be Emily. Maybe Emily's husband, Tom, would meet her. At this turbulent time for the family, Emily may simply have asked one of her many helpful friends to make the trip to the airport. *Great*, thought Deirdre cynically. After six hours on a plane, the last thing she wanted to do was make polite conversation with some Good Samaritan. Deirdre had left home before she had had time to find out who would be at Logan, leaving Jeremy to ensure that someone would, in fact, meet her. It was all up to Lady Luck – but Deirdre had always had a good relationship with her.

When she left the plane, the Jetway was packed with a crowd of departing passengers. The plane itself had been full. Despite her ease at getting a flight, it seemed the plane had no empty seats. She could only imagine that the New England foliage was a major magnet at this time of year. The sea of pent-up travelers the plane disgorged merged with even more people when it reached the terminal. It was rush hour at the airport. Airports are not places to go and idly dawdle. Rather, they are places to go with a definite purpose in mind. Still, everybody seemed to be moving slowly. She wanted to scream, "Get the lead out!" Like a football linebacker, she kept seeing daylight. But, also as in football, the room to maneuver would disappear as quickly as it appeared. Try as she might, she couldn't make any headway by weaving through the mass of people. She was very frustrated at everyone's apparent lack of concern for reaching his or her destination. Patience had never been her strong suit. In spite of the slow-moving crowd, she reached baggage claim fairly quickly. She had always thought that this airport was well laid out. Now she found that fact confirmed. Arriving passengers didn't have to travel far to retrieve their suitcases.

Deirdre spotted two slim brunettes on the outskirts of the crowd waiting for their luggage. Suspecting that they were her sisters, she was relieved to know she would be met by family and not by some stranger. As Deirdre got closer, she identified them as Emily and Penelope. They had both seen her and were waving. Both were dressed in conservative, navy dresses. Deirdre blushed at her clothing, really at the way she looked as a whole. She had traveled across the country in a pair of old corduroy pants and one of her oldest jerseys. Her corduroys were navy but worn and had definitely seen better days. She felt totally outclassed by her sisters' attire. But she'd known the six-hour flight would take a lot out of her. She couldn't imagine how she would feel if she were wearing uncomfortable clothes.

Her sisters' greetings weren't as effusive as they might have been under normal circumstances, but it was plain they were glad to see her.

Penelope asked, "How was your flight?"

Deirdre shot back, "Three thousand miles with a couple of whiny kids and the usual bad food, but it got me from there to here, so I shouldn't complain. Still, I can't pretend it wasn't a dreadful flight. I brought two rather large suitcases, so I hope you brought Tom's minivan."

Without letting Deirdre continue, Penelope answered, "We did bring the van. Caroline's flight arrives in a couple of hours. She's only staying a week, but she takes after Mother in the wardrobe department. Who knows how many suitcases she'll have?"

Deirdre resumed where she'd left off. "My suitcases are filled with every warm piece of clothing I own. It's just my luck that you guys are all bigger than me and wear bigger clothes. I can't borrow anything and will probably still have to go shopping for more warm clothes right away. Remember what Mark Twain reportedly said. 'The mildest winter I ever spent was summer in Puget Sound.' Well, you can say it another way as well. 'The chilliest summer I ever spent was winter in Puget Sound.' All my clothes are Puget Sound clothes. We don't have warm weather, but cold weather in the Northwest doesn't hold a candle to the severity of a New England winter."

"We are having unseasonably warm weather here, so you won't need to worry right away about warm clothes," Emily reassured her.

The bags soon started coming down the carousel. Deirdre volunteered, "My suitcases are green with leather trim. Should be easy to spot. You know me well enough to know I won't have the same black suitcases that everybody else does. I would rather be unique." Her bags were early, and she was right – it was hard to miss them. They were also big and fairly heavy. But they had wheels. When she attached the pull straps, Deirdre could easily pull the suitcases behind her.

The group had time to pass before Caroline's flight would arrive, so an airport lounge was the next destination. As with most airports, this one offered a number of convenient lounges to choose from. Since the airport was so crowded, it was not easy to find even one lounge with empty tables. But since airport lounge clientele didn't stay long, it wasn't long before the trio found a lounge where a table soon opened up. They knew, though, that they wouldn't have much time. With that in mind, they quickly ordered. Deirdre ordered her usual scotch, Penelope a whiskey sour; but since she was driving, Emily had ginger ale. Deirdre let off more steam about the flight, the noisy children, and the lousy food.

"I see you haven't stopped being a complainer," Emily said without hesitation.

Deirdre retorted, "You wouldn't be quite so critical if you'd been on that plane. Or if you weren't used to screaming children."

Emily glared at her. Bickering didn't seem like the best way to start out an extended stay, so they moved on to the events of the last few days.

Deirdre asked to be filled in about the plans for the coming week. Since Emily was on site and was handling the details, she did most of the talking. "Mother was doing last-minute shopping for the twins' birthday. She was in Webber's Department Store when she had the coronary. I don't know who, but someone called 911. It was too late by the time the ambulance arrived. You know that the sales girls at those stores are always young, particularly in a department for little kids. I feel so sorry for the one who was in the department Mother was in."

Deirdre didn't miss the chance to throw in her two cents. "It probably didn't do much for her commissions that day either." She had always been bad at remembering the twins' birthday, a fact that irritated Emily greatly. Now she had the chance to earn points with her sister. Deirdre seized the opportunity. "Bonnie and Ben must be nine. The time has just flown by. Hard to believe. We must be getting older. We certainly don't look it ..."

Emily looked at her gratefully. She could not believe her children's ages either. She felt that the years could not possibly show. At least, she felt that way.

Without realizing she was bringing the conversation back to the reason for their gathering, Penelope blurted out, "Well, you know what they say. At least Mother went quickly."

Emily saw the need to change the subject, finishing first with details about the funeral. "Mother always agreed with Daddy about cremation, so I've arranged that she be cremated. Mitchell's is handling it."

"Emily. Where are you gallivanting off to?" The question came out of the blue. Normally, it was unusual to run into anybody familiar in such an obscure location.

Emily turned toward the voice and recognized two old acquaintances. "This is an unlikely place to run into you two. Ted and Susan Williams, these are my sisters, Deirdre and Penelope." Looking at her sisters, Emily continued, "Ted and Susan and I are all veterans of the PTA at Molly's school."

It didn't surprise Deirdre a bit that these were PTA folks. Emily was so wrapped up in her children. It struck Deirdre that Emily had no other friends but people who had a direct connection to the kids or their school. Emily flashed Deirdre a look of irritation. Ted and Susan were obviously not among Emily's favorite people.

"Deirdre just flew in from Seattle. We're waiting for our other sister to arrive from DC. Where are you off to?" Emily tried to sound cheerful.

Ted and Susan blushed. It was clear that they had read the obituary in the paper, had not sent a card with their condolences, and were just now recognizing their faux pas. "We were so sorry to learn of your loss."

Emily carried the conversation forward, trying to eliminate the awkwardness. "Thank you. It was sudden, to say the least. We're all gathering in North Linton. Where are you going?"

Ted replied to the original question as Susan checked her watch, "We're stealing off to the Caribbean. You know, rates are really cheap at this time of year." It was obvious they didn't have much time before they needed to be on their plane. The need to end the conversation suited them because they were thoroughly embarrassed. It also suited Deirdre and her sisters because Caroline's flight would soon be arriving and they needed to get back to baggage claim before she showed up.

Back Emily, Deirdre, and Penelope went. Unfortunately, Deirdre's heavy suitcases had to make the trip back as well. At that point, it was decided that Emily would go get the car. All of the luggage could be loaded at the curb instead of dragging it across the parking lot. So off Emily went.

While Deirdre and Penelope waited, they speculated about Caroline's interpretation of the latest news from Capitol Hill. "The usual wrangling over the budget is in process right now. At least it's not a year when there are congressional elections. That always presents senators and representatives with a tough choice on the really tough issues." Deirdre's words showed at least a minimal awareness of the hurdles her sister faced.

Penelope concurred. "Caroline has her work cut out for her just monitoring regular legislation. In the grand scheme of things, negotiations over the budget only complicate the legislative process rather than making it easier. Gee, the girl herself should be here any minute."

Before long, Caroline was in front of them. Apparently, she too had flown on Screaming-Baby Airlines, but she was more composed than Deirdre had been. Alone among the four of them, Caroline had a tranquility about her that was enviable. Nobody knew for sure where it came from. When Emily and Deirdre had been teenagers, Caroline could read a book in the library and ignore a ringing phone. That had always enraged her older sisters, who believed that every phone call was of earth- shattering importance. That unflappable characteristic had, obviously, not changed.

Emily had been right to bring the van. Caroline had brought two medium-sized suitcases and a small one for toiletries and makeup. The use of makeup was another area where the sisters differed totally. Caroline was always dressed to the hilt and never went anywhere without makeup. Deirdre had never in her life worn any. They were both attractive young women. Caroline just worked at it harder. Now, like her sisters, she was clad in navy blue and wore a conservative linen dress with a crisp white collar. Deirdre wondered if Caroline had been at work. She would not put it past her sister to spend a day at the office before flying from DC to be with family. Perhaps her attire just reflected her refusal to be anywhere in public without spending at least an hour attending to her looks before leaving the house.

They retrieved her bags and went to the curbside with all the luggage to wait for Emily. They managed to get to the curb with little effort. While they waited somewhat impatiently, Deirdre and Penelope recounted the details of their mother's death and the funeral plans to Caroline. They shared their thoughts about the whole affair, agreeing that Emily should be treated with kid gloves, although they themselves were not overly aggrieved. While she did not have critical comments about her sisters' reactions to their bereavement, Caroline did have sharp words about Deirdre's attire. Deirdre defended herself by reminding Caroline that her own flight had been over three times as long. They had a congenial disagreement and then moved on to other, unrelated topics.

Emily took longer than they expected, but the van finally pulled up. Emily apologized for taking so long. Even though she had taken note of the row and space number when she'd parked the car, she had had trouble finding the row. The garage at the airport had been packed when she and Penelope had arrived. It was a true rabbit warren, and finding a space had been a challenge. They had been forced to park at some distance from the main terminal.

After Emily pulled the van closer to the curb, the sisters loaded the luggage and piled in. With all the bags, it was a tight fit despite the fact that it was a van. Without any discussion, Caroline got in front with Emily. Deirdre and Penelope got in back.

THE TRIP TO EMILY'S

THE VAN, LOADED WITH ALL FOUR SISTERS AND MORE luggage than Emily had anticipated, pulled away from the curb and headed on its way to North Linton. Looking out, Deirdre noticed that the orange barrels and sawhorses had disappeared. The last time she had been at Logan Airport, there had been construction everywhere. Now there was no sign of any disruption. Deirdre, however, did not recognize a thing. No congestion surrounded the airport, and none of the buildings she remembered was anywhere to be seen. Even the old transit station was gone. There was nothing familiar anywhere. Shortly after pulling out, they were suddenly traveling on a six-lane highway, heading north. Presto. The whole transition had been seamless.

But, where were the tunnels? Logan Airport had always been separated from the city by two tunnels, the Sumner and the Callahan. Deirdre could never remember which was which, but they had been symbolically important. They were sentinels to the magical world of travel. Deirdre had always felt, when she went through the entrance tunnel, that she was Alice falling down the rabbit hole. She had gone to wondrous places following the White Rabbit. Now it was just like the approach to any other airport in the States. Wonderland had lost some of its luster. Some of the mystery was gone, along with the tunnels. She had always thought Logan was different – special. To her, it always would be both.

The drive home was filled with comments about various landmarks and reminiscences about past trips over the years. The four women had only addressed the practical details of the reason for their gathering, not any emotional fallout. The death of their mother – Claire Lincoln – hung in the air as an unspoken presence. Instead of lingering on the topic at that point, they filled the time with general gossip, avoiding what they all knew would have to be dealt with at some later time. It was safer to pass the time with conversation about people and places. Soon enough, they would talk about what, if anything, they would miss and what holes might be created in their lives. But not yet. This was not something that any of them was terribly comfortable talking about so soon after her death. It had happened so recently that none of them had yet thought about what lingering emptiness they would have in their lives. They had varied relationships with her. They all knew their reactions to her passing were also varied now and were likely to continue that way for some time. So their mother's death remained an untouched subject.

"When I took the obituary for Mother to the Post, I

learned the town's latest news." Emily was anxious to share the scuttlebutt with her sisters. "The school committee has approved building a new high school. The old high school is no longer big enough. It will become the junior high. The town has really become the place to live. In addition to the normal growth, it is growing exponentially with all the new residents. Who would have thought our little burg would become such a mecca? I also learned that Patrick Flanagan died this week."

Flanagan was a town character and had led every town parade in his mint condition Model T for years. On chillier days, he had shown up in his raccoon coat, somewhat ratty in the later years.

"Did he make it to a hundred?" asked Penelope.

"No," answered Emily ruefully. "He was only ninety-eight."

Caroline piped up. "I guess the town will have to find somebody else to lead parades. Looks like an opening for a new generation. Maybe ours."

Deirdre's mind went back to the parades of their youth. "Do you guys remember marching in the parades?" A swarm of images flooded her mind – the girls with their scout troops lined up for celebrations of Memorial Day, the Fourth of July, and Labor Day. Turning to Caroline and Penelope, she added, "Of course, you two are so much younger. You were never in the parades Emily and I were in. I was only seven and a Brownie for my first parade."

Emily pontificated, "You were such a pip-squeak. You were exhausted but proud when Daddy collected us at the end. He was proud too and rewarded your efforts with an ice cream sundae."

"If I remember correctly, you got a sundae too," Deirdre reminded her.

That silenced Emily. Deirdre withdrew into herself and smiled broadly. Snippets of each parade brought old memories to light – a face here, a conversation there. As the memories swirled in her head, she found herself wondering what had become of some of the people she had not seen or heard about for years. Some were acquaintances she didn't care if she ever saw again. She wondered about them anyway. "Where is Andrea Scott these days? I was always jealous of her red hair. It was a rich, dark red. Beautiful."

Deirdre's sisters didn't know where this unexpected question came from and no one could answer it. Andrea had lived across the street from the cemetery that was the destination for the Memorial Day parade. Whenever Deirdre thought of those parades, she still mused about what had become of Andrea. It had never helped, of course, that Andrea was smart as well as pretty.

The parades brought warm memories to Deirdre's mind. She was sure the memories were much better than they had actually been. After the summer parades, the town held a huge picnic and barbecue on the town green. The green was big enough to accommodate anyone who wanted to attend. One year, the person in charge of potato salad had been less than fastidious. There had been a rash of cases of food poisoning after the picnic. Deirdre had learned from that experience never to eat potato salad that had not been made by someone she personally knew. She'd actually learned many things from those experiences. None of the lessons was as practical as the one involving mayonnaise. Most were social or behavioral, but all had a major impact on how she lived her life. She had fine-tuned her courtesy, patience, and tolerance at those gatherings. Obviously, the lessons about patience hadn't lasted long. She had also developed a passion for barbecued chicken. That had lasted. Jeremy never quite understood the foundation for her insistence on buying a rotisserie. He had acquiesced without too much resistance though.

Deirdre snapped back to the present when Emily threw in her final bit of news. Emily's mischievous grin indicated she knew her sisters would be as scandalized as she had been. "Do you remember Maureen Doran from my class in high school? Well, she just had her eighth kid. No wonder they're building a new high school!"

Without any discussion, Emily started heading on a route that would take them past what had been a favorite haunt for them growing up – Harry's Deli. The deli had a small number of comfortable tables, all equipped with cribbage boards and decks of cards. Aside from being a great eating establishment, it had been a good hangout. The deli served a limited number of sandwiches on site, but offered a much bigger selection of foods to buy for home consumption. Deirdre often found herself thinking of those sandwiches and missing them – no, yearning for one. There would be no cribbage tonight, but Deirdre knew they would at least all order delicious pastrami sandwiches and potato salad. Dill pickles were optional, a matter of individual choice, but they would all finish their meals with Harry's signature cheesecake. It was too good to pass up.

When they finally got to Harry's Deli, the parking

lot was almost empty. It was near closing time. Deirdre was crestfallen. She had been so looking forward to a pastrami sandwich. She thought how insignificant such a desire was, considering the events that had brought them all together, but at this point her stomach overruled her mind. She was focused on that sandwich.

"Harry has turned the business over to his son Julian, but the food is as good as it's always been." Emily reported this happily.

Deirdre perked up. "I was worried there for a minute. I feel better now."

They scrambled out of the van, hoping they would not be too late. When they got inside, they were delighted to see Harry himself behind the counter. Harry looked up and broke into a grin when they walked in. "Well, if it isn't the Lincoln girls." They had been customers for so long that they thought of him in the same way one would think of a favorite uncle. Like all uncles, he had aged and lost his thinning hair. The wrinkles on his face were now permanent signs of many years of laughter.

He obviously thought of the girls as more than just run-of-the-mill customers. "What will it be? The usual for all of you?" Harry had a remarkable memory. "So, what brings you all here at once?"

There was an awkward pause. Then Emily said, "My sisters have come home for Mother's funeral."

Harry's sympathy was genuine. "I'm so sorry to hear that. What a loss. The world will be a poorer place without her."

How charitable. If you only knew what she thought of you, thought Deirdre to herself.

Harry chatted on, "I'm lucky I was here to see you.

Em probably told you that Julian is now running the business. I'm only here because his wife is out tonight and he had to be home babysitting."

"I think we're the lucky ones." Deirdre meant every word.

They ordered and ate without much delay, knowing that Tom would be expecting them. It was a short visit, but not a trip went by without a stop at Harry's Deli.

After bidding a reluctant farewell for such a short stay, the sisters piled back into the van and continued to wend their way homeward. The driving was slower on the roads they chose than on the main thoroughfares, but the shortcuts they knew actually made the drive faster. When they got close to Emily's house, they drove through a wooded area. Deirdre had gotten soil for one of her science fair projects from one of the bogs near there. The land on either side of the road was boggy. The bogs, by their very nature, could never be built on. That meant it would be forever wilderness. Not much had changed, and not much ever would. That fact always made Deirdre happy.

Then the bog was behind them. As suddenly as they had left it, they were faced with the Atlantic Ocean raging against the granite rocks. The transition was dramatic. A sense of being home quickly settled in.

It wasn't far to Emily's house now. She and Tom had built their first house on what had once been the outskirts of town. They'd only lived in that house a short time before they moved to an oceanfront property. The house they moved to had been built in the 1840s by a sea captain for his wife. It struck Deirdre that this woman had lived a life remarkably similar to that of her mother. They'd both lived widows' lives without actually being widows. Deirdre thought of the place on the roof where Molly was only allowed to play when one of her parents was with her. That was the vista that the sea captain's wife had seen when he was sailing and the one to which she had retreated for solace after the sea finally claimed her husband.

After the long drive from the airport, they finally pulled into Emily and Tom's driveway. This *new* old house was closer to the center of town than the previous one had been. The town was continuing to expand, with new developments being built farther removed from the town center than the housing development where their first house had been. Emily and Tom had been lucky to find a house closer to the bustling town core. And it now bustled more and more.

The motion-sensitive light by the driveway flickered on as they drove in. Tom, a little bit anxious at their lateness, came out of the house to meet them when he heard the van pull in. The twins were already in bed, but Molly, eager to see her aunts again, had stayed up, waiting for them to get home. She had her pajamas on and, demure in the way that only girls in their early adolescence can be, stayed inside.

The foursome spilled out of the van. The day had tired all of them, but in different ways. Only Deirdre was still in a different time zone. They left it to Tom to bring in the bags, while the two weary travelers mustered enthusiasm to greet their niece. It was unclear who was the most exhausted. The mental strain had taken a toll on all four of them. Molly seemed to be in the best shape of the group. It wasn't long before they went off to their respective beds. To make room for this onslaught of guests, Emily had rearranged the sleeping accommodations in the house. Bonnie had vacated her room and was sleeping with Molly. Deirdre and Penelope would share Bonnie's room. Bowing to necessity, Tom had moved in with Ben, leaving room for Caroline to share the bed in the master bedroom with Emily.

Everyone gratefully said their goodnights and turned in. That left Tom to lock up and join little Ben, who had never even woken up. The next few days would be as difficult for him as for his wife and her sisters, but in physical rather than emotional ways. The Lincolns needed each other's company. Deirdre was glad they were together once again.

Baking the Quiches

Emily, Caroline, and Penelope were busy in the kitchen when Deirdre struggled downstairs. The previous day had been a long one for both Caroline and Deirdre, but Deirdre had flown six hours while Caroline had only had a two-hour flight. Though Deirdre was used to waking up early, she was exhausted from the cross-country trip and slept late that morning. She had crossed three time zones, but was still on Pacific Time. With thoughts of yesterday's arduous trip in mind, her sisters had kindly let her sleep in. They had left muffins, butter, and jam on the table, ready for when Deirdre finally did rouse herself.

All three of her sisters were at the counter when she made her appearance. They had their backs to the kitchen table, so they did not notice Deirdre slip in. Her slippers were soft and padded, allowing her to move without a sound. It looked to Deirdre as though Emily, Caroline, and Penelope, hunched over the counter, were operating in an assembly line. Deirdre sat at the table, watching them work together effortlessly, before she said anything. She started to eat a muffin and then turned to brightly greet them. "What are you making over there?" She was curious about what could be occupying them so intently.

Deirdre knew she could expect a straightforward answer and not questions about how she'd slept.

Emily didn't disappoint and responded quickly to her sister's inquiry. "People are likely to congregate in the parish hall after the funeral. It will be just after noon, and they'll be hungry. There will be a simple luncheon for them to eat. The one thing Mother was very successful at was instilling courtesy in us all."

Penelope threw in, "She sure wasn't good at making quiches. Or much else."

Emily picked up her description of the funeral lunch. "As we all know, Mother was a lousy cook. Unlike her quiches, these will be good. I figure we need to make twelve of them. Aunt Miriam is making enough green salad to feed the Russian army."

Deirdre now knew about the main course. "Yeah, but what about the rest of it?"

Penelope answered, "Stephanie Lewis is providing brownies, and Ginny Finch will take care of beverages."

Deirdre turned back to her breakfast. As she was eating, she looked around the room. "It looks as though you've remodeled the kitchen since I was here last."

Emily turned, bubbling over and flushing. "We did. And we splurged and bought cherry cupboards. The tiles on the walls are custom made too."

Deirdre raised her eyebrows imperceptibly. "I see

that all the appliances are new. And talk about splurging. Granite countertops?"

Each room in this house had been remodeled as the inspiration struck Emily. All the redecorating reflected a lot of attention to detail, nothing more so than in this updated kitchen. It was clear that a lot of money had been spent in the whole process. Tom owned two sporting goods stores, and they were, obviously, doing quite well.

The dining room showed evidence that Emily and Tom were frequent entertainers. Emily made good use of the china she'd received as a wedding present. At the time, Deirdre had not been able to imagine what all that fancy stuff would be used for. She still knew she would never have great use for that kind of tableware in her home or life. But she realized that Emily's life had an entirely different center. Upon reflection, she saw that the difference was in more than just their decorating style. They were affected by their mother's death, as they had been by her life, in markedly different ways. Even though both represented the early years of Claire and Derek's marriage, Deirdre's and Emily's experiences were not at all the same. The wide variation in the way they felt showed that.

As she resumed her survey of the rooms she could see from where she sat, she once again was struck by the contrast in how she and her older sister lived their lives. This could be seen in the way the living room was appointed. It was another fairly formal room, with a luxurious Oriental rug and a number of wing chairs. She assumed their mother's piano would end up at Emily's house and was surprised there wasn't already a piano in the living room. Deirdre could envision the grand piano in that room. As she mentally went through the house, she found herself wondering how she and Emily could possibly have grown up together. Actually, all four of the Lincoln girls had such entirely different tastes. How could any of them have come from the same household? The differences had not been apparent when they were teens. In contrast, Emily's children showed the beginnings of different tastes.

Her kids' bedrooms had been refurbished early on to reflect their changing interests. Molly was now at the age when pink was just too juvenile. She had nagged so much that Emily had felt she had no choice but to repaint the room a soft cream and furnish it entirely anew. Molly had reached a level of increased *sophistication*. Her room was now outfitted with *grown-up* accessories. It didn't have curtains or a rug. It had drapes and a carpet – well, there was a rug, but it was an Oriental one. The new color scheme had eggplant accents. Ben's room had recently been decorated with wallpaper that featured football helmets. Emily said she had shuddered all day when the wallpaper went up, but she assumed, and fervently hoped, this phase would not last long. Bonnie, meanwhile, was enamored with horses. Her room was easy to decorate. All that had been required were lamps with horses on them, appropriate pictures of Kentucky horse farms, a horseshoe on the wall, and a few freestanding horse figures in the bookcase. *An easy child,* Deirdre thought. *One out of three isn't bad.*

Deirdre glanced over at her sisters. Judging by their casual attire, there were no plans to go anywhere that day.

Emily never wore blue jeans, but she was wearing what looked like her oldest slacks. With a horrified thought, Deirdre realized Emily really was looking her age – that of a middle-aged parent. Caroline wore tailored blue jeans and a striking neckerchief, probably a silk one. True to form, she was impeccably turned out. Deirdre wondered if she were ever otherwise. She felt that her distance from Caroline was even broader than her distance from Emily. She turned her gaze to Penelope, who, wearing only black at the symphony, had now added an unexpected flash of color with a red jersey, albeit a subdued red. Looking at Penelope made Deirdre feel, once again, that she was on familiar territory.

It was fitting that all four would spend the day together at Emily's home. There was a lot to talk about, both past and future. Having been working at the counter for quite some time, the three sisters left what they had begun that morning and joined Deirdre at the table for tea. There was a definite family resemblance between those three. All four looked like their mother, but Emily, Caroline, and Penelope also had a strong likeness to their father. Deirdre had always been jealous of her sisters. Derek had had fine, chiseled features that made him stand out in a crowd. Three of his daughters had inherited the best of his looks. Of the four, only Deirdre had her mother's blonde hair. These days, even that had some help. The other three were brunettes with hair of various lengths. Emily, Caroline, and Penelope were tall, while Deirdre was petite. She had always wished she were statuesque like her sisters, but she suspected she might benefit from her small stature now when their mother's wardrobe came into the picture.

Over cups of tea, they brought each other up to date on what was going on in their lives. Emily talked about her three kids, who were the center of her life. They were growing by leaps and bounds. Molly was now twelve and approaching those treacherous teenage years. She was a great student, was becoming a very good pianist, and was a regular volunteer at a local soup kitchen. She was also already interested in boys. As everyone knows, adolescents can easily veer off course at that age. Who knows where their fancies will take them next? Emily was worried that Molly would lose the great gains she seemed to be making in her studies and in her music.

The twins were just starting fourth grade and were, more and more, going their own separate ways, as twins of different sexes tend to do at that age. After that, Emily talked about her own foibles. She, herself, had reached a plateau in her life. She was branching out from her newspaper column and starting to write short stories, already amassing a number, with ideas for more tumbling in her head. She was not yet sure what to do with them but thought she would like to publish a book. She elicited suggestions about topics from her sisters and listened closely to what they had to offer.

Deirdre talked excitedly about how the nursery business was doing. She had become entranced with flowering shrubs in the past year. A much greater variety was successful in the Pacific Northwest, despite the rain. Or maybe because of it. That had opened up a greater gardening avenue for her. New England may have a corner on autumn, but there is nothing like springtime in the Northwest. She felt she was justifying being so far away from the rest of the family. Before the plane had landed at Logan, she knew she would enjoy being with her family again, despite the circumstances. Still, there really was nothing she would rather do than lose herself in a Northwest garden.

Parenthetically, she added, "We're very lucky it's fall. The nursery business is winding down for the winter. Jeremy's presence is still needed though. He's overseeing a few end-of-season odds and ends – the bulb sale, the perennial sale, preparing the nursery, and placing orders for the Christmas season and what little we will need for the winter months." Jeremy would fly east for Thanksgiving, entrusting the business to their capable manager.

For her part, Caroline spoke quietly but fervently. "I'm doing litigation involving water quality in the southeast. Very little environmental legislation exists in the states in that part of the country, so we have to fall back on federal legislation. I'm optimistic about how it will turn out." She always had Jon in the background cheering her on whenever her spirits started to flag.

When it was her turn, Penelope volunteered her comments enthusiastically. "I am currently learning the flute part in the violin concerto by Mendelssohn. The orchestra is planning to add the concerto to its repertoire in the upcoming season. I'm relieved that I only have one new piece to learn this year." Orchestras usually added more than one piece to their repertoire each year. The gods were smiling on Penelope. The Lincoln family often had the Mendelssohn Violin Concerto, among many other classical pieces, playing in the background, so all the girls could recognize it in a flash. Playing any of it was something else again. None of the rest of them could even dream of attempting to play it. In addition, the flute was not a distinctive instrument in the concerto. It presented a particular challenge for Penelope.

As they concluded their brief summaries, Deirdre finished her breakfast. "A muffin is more than enough for me as long as I can snack throughout the afternoon." She then joined her sisters as they returned to the counter. They each had a job in the assembling process. It had been a long time since they had cooked together, but it came back easily. Their teamwork was flawless. It came from a lot of years of experience. Emily had taken over responsibility for dinner when she sixteen. Each of the sisters, when she was old enough, had started by helping with minor tasks. Each had taken on increasing responsibility and, eventually, moved into the role of head chef when her sister had vacated that role. The job of head chef had proven to be a great preparation for adulthood.

In the course of the day, they spent a lot of time reminiscing. Odd bits of their childhood, random moments, floated past each one and came to light. Deirdre remembered learning to ride a bicycle. "Remember the big hilly park in the center of town? Daddy took me there one afternoon when I was about six. There was, after all, no traffic. It was the perfect place for a kid to practice and wobble, fall down, and then get up and try again. We spent the entire afternoon there. By the end of the day, I was riding like a trooper." After that, it wasn't long before she'd moved on to a much bigger bicycle, but she would never feel quite the same about any other bike as she had about that first little black one. The sense of freedom when she'd gotten rid of those training wheels had been the first of many such liberating moments in her life. Just thinking about it brought a big smile to her face.

Emily recalled the days of going to the candy store. When they were little, their allowances had been a dime a week, a lot in those days when ten cents would buy a lot of candy. "I didn't know the name then, but the dime made me feel like John D. Rockefeller. I used to spend fifty minutes deciding how that dime would be spent. The women at the candy store, without a doubt the wives of the owners, were kindly and patient. I'd carefully select my allotment of candy for the month. That was where I developed my passion for malted milk balls." That month's other dimes were destined for the piggy bank.

Then there was the subject of twins. Emily and Deirdre first learned about twins when they had met grown sisters who lived near each other and the Lincolns. These women looked just like each other. Imagine that. Just before Caroline was born, and again before Penelope was born, their mother had explained that they were getting a new sister or brother soon. The topic of twins was avidly discussed, in whispers, by Emily and Deirdre after the lights went out. Based on having met the twin sisters, Deirdre decided she wanted two. And they had to look exactly the same. Needless to say, her hopes were dashed at Caroline's birth. And again when Penelope was born and she too was alone.

So many happy memories went back to times before

the two younger girls had been old enough to share in the escapades of their older sisters. Deirdre was clear in her recollection of one particular event. "I'll never forget the vacation we took to Mt. Washington. I agreed with Mother about that one. I know Daddy was a frustrated outdoorsman, but I still think it was a bit much to make a four-year-old climb the tallest mountain in New England, never mind on a trail as hard as Tuckerman's Ravine. Mother was as sluggish as I was, but unbeknownst to anyone, including her, she was pregnant with Caroline. To this day, I wonder if I hold the record for the youngest person to climb Mt. Washington. Then again, no one is keeping a record, so I'll just have to think I do hold it." Deirdre felt a bit smug.

Emily lit up, smiling with recollections of another vacation. "Then there was the summer we went to that resort near Mount Monadnock. Another one of Daddy's harebrained ideas. That time, Mother was not as accommodating. The vacation started well, but there were too many mosquitoes. They bit me mercilessly. They did a number on Caroline too, poor kid. We both itched without relief. When Mother and Daddy left us with that woman to go off for the afternoon, I slept for most of the time and then woke up and threw up all over the place. I was not popular."

Caroline blurted out indignantly. "Too many? One mosquito is too many."

"Is that why you live in DC?" Emily asked.

Deirdre turned to Emily. "Do you remember the time Daddy took us out to lunch that Easter Sunday?" It stood out in her mind as one of the best holidays ever. "I must have been eleven or twelve. I know I had baked stuffed lobster for the first time. That was an expensive and stupid mistake on his part. He had to buy me lobster from then on whenever we went out to eat, without complaining."

"I had steak." Emily beamed as if it happened last week. "I never got over your Easter hat that year – that broad-brimmed straw hat with the long, green streamers. I wanted it so badly. I could not figure out why you had a better hat than I did. I was, after all, older."

Deirdre remembered her Easter outfit too. "I loved the coat that went with that hat. That's right. I was eleven. They don't make coats like that anymore, even for grown-ups. It's probably because Easters aren't as chilly as they used to be." A few years later, Caroline had worn that same dress. She'd outgrown it faster than Deirdre had. Both Caroline and Penelope grew so much faster than Deirdre. When each one was fourteen, she was taller. It made the term *little sister* irrelevant.

Those little sisters listened as Emily and Deirdre took turns telling stories they had heard countless times but were not likely to hear again. From early childhood, Caroline and Penelope had each had an older sister she had come to regard as, and who was, in fact, a guardian. The older sister was, for each, a mentor.

When Caroline had been still a toddler, the eleven-year-old Emily had taken it upon herself to oversee Caroline's upbringing. When Caroline outgrew clothes or shoes, Emily saw to it that she got new ones. Dentist appointments were not overlooked either. At the start, Emily's oversight was like having a new doll to play with, but it soon became a serious responsibility. Then when

Penelope had come along, Deirdre had done the same with her. From those early years, the four had developed bonds – Emily with Caroline, Deirdre with Penelope. Those bonds had been strengthened throughout their lives. So, instead of the two older sisters and the two younger sisters being close, there were two older/younger sister pairs.

As they continued to talk, Deirdre was surprised to learn that her sisters' fondest memories, like hers, happened before the age of five. It turned out that all four had images of their first days of school, even picturing the clothes they wore the first day. Without mentioning specific details, they each had rosy memories of that day. But it seemed that their mother had become less interested in them as they began to think for themselves. The happy times were about to be supplanted by the start of minor skirmishes.

Deirdre went back to her first confrontation with her mother. It wasn't a pleasant memory, but it was certainly one that indicated the future. She had gone to her first dance at age fourteen and snuck nylons to wear in her purse. Even though she had been smart enough to take them off, she had not been smart enough to take them out of her purse. She'd been caught red-handed. Or was that red-footed? While she had not won entirely, she had not exactly lost either. It was clear that her mother did not have strong fiber – or at least that hers wasn't as strong as Deirdre's. Each of the girls had had a somewhat similar experience. The circumstances were different, but the end result was the same – a compromise at best.

Deirdre had turned to various teachers, in particular

her fifth grade teacher, for the kind of reinforcement she needed. That wonderful woman had taken her under her wing at a time when Deirdre had been especially in need of positive attention. Her teacher had taught her, more than even her father had, about the importance of critical thinking, something that had always seemed beyond her mother's capabilities. Deirdre was sad that her mother had never experienced the freedom that kind of thinking brought. Deirdre had begun to hone her abilities in that respect, but only then had she started to realize how different she and her mother were. That was the beginning of a gap between them that never closed. Deirdre looked back on her relationship with her mother with regret. The breach had only widened with time and distance. She blamed herself as much as her mother. She knew that her sisters had issues with their mother as well. She just didn't know how deep those rifts were. Another topic to explore during the week.

THE YOUNGER SISTERS

CAROLINE LET IT BE KNOWN TO HER SISTERS THAT SHE preferred the term *demise* to *death*. She was in denial. The quiches they were making would be served at a luncheon in celebration of her mother's life. Her mother, herself, inexplicably could not attend. It was all part of Caroline's grand self-deception. True, Caroline had chosen to live at a distance from North Linton. Emily had privately told Deirdre that was no accident. True, Caroline only made infrequent visits to her hometown. Deirdre suspected that was intentional too. But Caroline didn't seem ready to make things permanent yet. They were, of course, already that way, but Caroline showed no readiness to admit it.

In accord with what her mother would have done, Caroline had spent the day before flying to Boston shopping for clothes suitable for a funeral and bereavement in general. She had also picked up a few new dresses and scarves just for good measure. The clothes, though, were not of the style her mother would have chosen. Only the price tags were. Caroline's tastes were much more contemporary. They had been that way since Caroline had moved to Washington. In that respect, she differed from her sisters as much as from her mother. It was not the only way she stood out from her sisters. All the Lincoln daughters were striking, but Caroline was truly beautiful. Her long auburn tresses shone and were softly wavy; her large eyes bordered on green; her skin was clear and almost translucent. Like two of her sisters, she had high cheekbones and that distinctive Lincoln nose.

Claire had wanted Caroline to enter the fashion industry after college graduation, either as a high-paid model or as a designer. It really didn't matter to Claire which. She did not take into consideration that her second youngest daughter's mind was as sharp as her looks were enchanting. They had all inherited their father's brains, but Caroline was the smartest by far. Emily had a way with words, but Caroline could be eloquent in both speech and writing. Deirdre's strength was in biology; Caroline excelled in every scientific branch. Penelope stood out in music; Caroline's spirit was lyrical.

By the end of her third year in college, Caroline had decided that she should follow the inclination that had been growing ever stronger throughout her college years. In her senior year, she'd applied to law school. Being a lawyer could be combined with another strong interest she had picked up unconsciously from her father. Law and politics went together well. The apple didn't fall far from the tree, but one side of that tree could be very different from the other. Derek and Claire had very different interests and had opposing ideas about

Caroline's future. It had never occurred to either one that what they wanted was not really relevant. Caroline's choice of vocation was the biggest disagreement between Claire and Caroline as well. Caroline only nodded to fashion when it came to personal appearance, not profession.

Caroline had her own life, her own circle of friends. She met Jon when both of their organizations were battling a particularly odious piece of congressional legislation. When they were unsuccessful in that effort, Caroline and Jon got together to strategize about cases that could be brought before the courts in order to find that legislation unconstitutional. They were thrown together for many days during that endeavor, and when they were successful finding cases for a potential challenge, the champagne they shared was not just a celebratory bottle. Shortly thereafter, she and Jon flew to Hartford and, in the presence of Penelope and a few college friends, were married in the magnificent Trinity Chapel. Postponing a real honeymoon, they spent a long weekend at a nearby bed-and-breakfast before returning to Washington to resume their ongoing fight against further Congressional insults.

When Claire and Derek learned Caroline and Jon had tied the knot, neither one was pleased – Derek, because he'd missed the chance to escort Caroline down the aisle, Claire, because she'd missed the chance to entertain a large crowd. For Claire, everything was subjective. Caroline's feelings were only secondary.

Deirdre was the only family member to be unreservedly happy about Caroline's marriage to Jon. She knew that the couple's happiness was what really counted. Emily and Penelope were both too wrapped up in their individual concerns to be much affected by the drama of Caroline's marriage.

The parents soon got used to visiting Caroline and Jon in their small apartment close to Rock Creek Park. While the art museums in the district were big attractions for Claire, sitting in the gallery above the House of Representatives mesmerized Derek. Those periodic visits continued through numerous changes in residence before Caroline and Jon settled in a modest house. Derek only visited them one time in their house before his untimely death. Claire's visits continued.

Derek's death had hit Caroline hard. Losing a parent had never crossed her mind before. She had become wrapped up in all the ins and outs of her job and had little time for matters unrelated to work. Her father's death caused her to slow down. She had just been getting back in the full swing of things, and now Claire's sudden passing put her back in the mode of grieving. The full import of that event would only penetrate the exterior shell of her tranquility later.

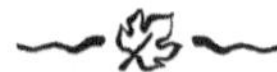

Penelope's reaction to their mother's death lay somewhere between Caroline's and Deirdre's. She was not quite as unwilling to accept reality as Caroline and less willing than Deirdre. She was the youngest of the four daughters, the last to remain at home. She was the last recipient of the attention her mother lavished on her daughters, if lavish could be used to describe Claire's attention. As far as Deirdre was concerned, the word interfere was more appropriate to the way Claire treated Penelope.

Penelope had only been eleven when Deirdre had left for college. That was Emily's final year in college. Even though Caroline was still in high school and therefore still at home, the house had seemed empty for the entire year. Caroline had always kept more to herself rather than spending time with any of her sisters. Her solitary habit continued even after Deirdre left for school. She still barely spent any time with her younger sister. Penelope was forced to learn, in Deirdre's absence, how to look out for her own interests.

Deirdre had always taken care of Penelope, both physically and emotionally. Deirdre chose Penelope's clothes, making sure she didn't freeze in winter or sweat inordinately in summer. It went without saying, of course, that if you lived in New England you were going to sweat in summer. The emotional part of life was a bit harder. Penelope owed Deirdre a lot for helping her over some emotional shoals. With her big sister's absence, she'd been forced to explore and develop hitherto neglected aspects of herself. Out of the whole experience, Penelope had become a stronger person. Thinking back on what had been an otherwise very lonely time, she was grateful for the opportunities she'd had to branch out. Among other things, she had started to devote more time to the flute. Taking her music more seriously had turned out to be very important to her. It had led to where she was today. She'd started to spend much more time on other of her studies, as well. She'd become a wizard at math, which, for some reason, had proved to have a symbiotic relationship with music. She had also become proficient at the French language. Language studies also seemed to use the same parts of the brain as music studies.

During the year when the two oldest girls were away at college, Penelope and Caroline had become closer. It was not an emotional closeness, merely a surface one. Penelope did not have a lot of friends in high school. Caroline, on the other hand, had many friends in school. In that time period, Penelope relied on Caroline to help her over the bumps that being a teenager presented. With Caroline's help, Penelope became more adept in social situations. Caroline even tried to get Penelope to spend more time on her looks. Penelope started paying more attention to her clothing and styled her thick brown hair in a new fashion but drew the line at makeup. Deirdre's influence was obviously at work here, even from afar. Penelope turned out to be well-dressed but in a much more casual way – another difference from Caroline in wavelength. With all of the coaching in her favor, Penelope managed to survive high school – and fairly well, if not easily.

When Emily graduated from college, she never really came home to stay. Her return was only temporary. She and Tom were engaged. There was a wrinkle, though. Tom was in graduate school. They were waiting for him to get his master's degree before they were married. The two years after Emily came home were a continuous flurry of prewedding plans. Emily was attentive to her two younger sisters but had her mind on a wide variety of other things. The usual elements on a bride's mind – dress, registering, presents, thank-you notes – took precedence over everything else.

The wedding itself took place in the summer before Deirdre returned to college for her final year. The fact that the wedding and the plans in the year leading up to it were finally over turned out to be a big relief for everyone in the family, especially Penelope. By that time, Penelope was quite bored with the whole affair. But when the newlyweds came home, Penelope threw herself into helping her big sister set up household. This, at least, was a new and interesting project.

To Penelope's disappointment, Deirdre never came home at all after she graduated. Deirdre spent her first postcollege years living in, working in, and exploring Rhode Island. It fitted the bill by being a locale that was distant from North Linton while still being part of New England.

That was also the year that Caroline went to college, and Penelope was really alone. She was now the only daughter in the Lincoln household. Visiting Deirdre on the occasional weekend and during school vacations helped enliven Penelope's days but did little else. For the first time, she was enjoying the benefits of being the youngest, and the only daughter at home. Her father had decided to spend the time he had previously devoted to Deirdre on her instead. Her mother had never quite stopped regarding Penelope as the baby. There were innumerable times when Penelope was exasperated by her mother's attitude toward her, but in those early high school days, she was still raw enough to appreciate the added attention, especially since her sisters were gone. The parts of her that were increasingly independent helped her survive her mother's condescension and get her through the stress caused by that attitude. Parts of her appreciated the begrudging attention.

By the time she got to college, she was more of an independent spirit than any of her sisters had been at that age. At the end of college, she was more than ready to venture on new, as-yet-untraveled paths. None of her sisters had struck out as completely as she did. For that fact alone, she earned their respect, if not admiration. She felt she had finally surmounted the *little girl* position she had been relegated to by their mother. Going to New York after she'd graduated was another facet of that independence.

Penelope was just growing tired of New York when the job with the orchestra fell into her lap. That had happened just days after her father's funeral. Wouldn't he be proud! Her sisters were already settled on their paths. She had been relieved that she wouldn't end up as a little lost sheep.

THE FUNERAL

EMILY'S KITCHEN BUSTLED WITH ACTIVITY SATURDAY morning. It started with Tom, shirtsleeves rolled up and an uncharacteristic floral apron over his suit pants, cooking oatmeal for the twins. He had awakened them early because they would be spending the day with playmates who lived nearby. The playmates' mother had generously offered to look after the twins during the funeral and for as long as necessary afterward.

By the time Deirdre got downstairs, everyone else was already down there. Deirdre was fully dressed. There were still a few additional pieces of clothing for Emily and Penelope to add to their outfits. Molly, who would be going with them, still needed a lot of sartorial guidance. Caroline, wearing a borrowed housecoat, had already done her makeup but had yet to put on the clothes she would wear to the service. Deirdre knew that they did not have a lot of time to fritter away and was, therefore, prepared to go light on eating. She didn't want any action of hers to make them late. Nobody else but Tom seemed to be concerned about the clock. She sensed that Tom was thinking the same way she was. Deirdre could only trust that things would all work out.

After finishing cooking the twins' breakfast, Tom put on his tie and the suit jacket he'd casually left on a living room chair. He gathered up the quiches they had made the previous day and then loaded them in a cooler, ready to transport to the church kitchen. After that, he escorted the twins to the neighbor's house, hoping they would have a better day than the one he knew was in store for him.

Meanwhile, everyone disappeared upstairs to finish dressing. They soon magically reappeared, ready to go. Deirdre was surprised by the alacrity with which the final preparations had transpired. Still, they barely had enough time to get to the church. Tom, Emily, Molly, and all the food went in one car. Deirdre, Caroline, and Penelope went in the other one. Nobody was sure what to expect.

Arriving at the church, they discovered that the parking lot was full. While the church itself was not packed, they found that a lot of people were in attendance. A quick glance told Deirdre that she recognized many faces. There was substantial representation from the church's women's auxiliary and from the country club, the bridge club, the garden club, and the social circle that Claire had traveled in. Emily's face showed disappointment at the small size of the crowd. Deirdre, on the other hand, was pleasantly surprised. It was a classic glass half-empty/half-full dichotomy.

A meeting with the minister before entering the sanctuary was requisite in order to confirm the content of the service. Then the family followed him to the front pews. It struck Deirdre that it was a macabre variation of a wedding – the family enters last and sits up front. They settled into the whole row, with Molly sitting between her mother and Deirdre. Deirdre grabbed Molly by the hand and gave it a reassuring squeeze.

Molly had never been to a funeral before and was grateful for the support. She already missed her grandmother, even though she, in the past, had often resented Claire's interference.

None of the sisters was a regular churchgoer, but all four had intermittent experience to draw on. Each one knew how the service should go. When the girls were little, Derek and Claire had thought that their daughters should have some religious exposure. It made sense from a societal perspective. Derek and Claire had taken turns driving the girls to church when their daughters were young, turning around and driving right back home as soon as they dropped their charges off. Deirdre caught on early and often developed a "headache," causing the head of the Sunday school to call her parents up. Then one of them would have to drive back to fetch her. Deirdre felt it served them right.

A subdued murmur rippled through the church, quieting down as the funeral service began. So did Deirdre's nerves. From her father's funeral, she remembered all the words of the Episcopal service – the resurrection and the life and the rest of the phrases that are palliatives. Deirdre was amazed at herself for needing the consolation, but she was grateful that the words were there. The service pretty much followed what they had previously discussed with the minister. Reverend Blewitt had found an appropriate passage in Matthew. Deirdre was happy to get away from the gospel of John. To her, John was just too bleak. This was certainly not the time to be glad, but the Sermon on the Mount was far more appropriate, if not to their mother's life, at least to their own mind-sets. There was a simple humility to Matthew and his whole message.

Both Uncle David and Emily gave eulogies. David talked more about Claire's early life from the perspective of an older brother. It was clear that losing a younger sister had taken a great toll on him. The bond between them had remained strong, despite the many challenges that had strained their relationship over the years. He spoke glowingly of her. His talk minimized the traits that others could only describe as tart or, in the best case, difficult.

Emily held herself together and expressed her thoughts movingly. "I am speaking for my sisters and, I know, for all of you when I say that Mother will be sorely missed. You never knew quite when she would pop into your life, but you could always count on the fact that it would happen soon. And it was always a delightful happening. I'm sorry my children only had a few years of that presence."

The hymns were ones whose scores were written by well-known classical composers. Derek's influence was, remotely, at work here. Or was it Penelope's? The last music was a piece exclusively of bell ringing. It was surprisingly soothing. Penelope definitely had her hand in there. Somehow, she had known it would be a fitting end for the service.

When the service finished, Deirdre felt a surge of relief

that it was over. The family all trooped out, preceding the rest of the congregation. The event mirrored a wedding once more as the family left the main part of the church, exited to the parish hall, and formed a receiving line. Deirdre recognized so many of the people as they passed through the line. It was like watching a kaleidoscope of her youth. First came old Mrs. Chambers. She had lived next door for years. Her appearance surprised Deirdre, who would have thought her mother would have attended Mrs. Chambers's funeral, not the other way around. Mrs. Chambers looked like she was still going strong. She had been old when, seventeen years earlier, she had given Emily the wedding present of personally handwoven place mats. Deirdre considered it the perfect definition of a wedding present. She regretted that she, herself, had not received the same present when she was married, but she and Jeremy had sent very few invitations and had a very low-key wedding. Still, she was jealous. That present couldn't be matched. It would be the perfect gift for any future wedding she was invited to. If only she could weave – which, of course, she couldn't.

Next through the receiving line came a group of acquaintances from the bridge club. Deirdre didn't know if her mother had continued to play bridge regularly, but if she had, her foursome would have to find a new partner, not an easy job at that age. In Deirdre's youth, her mother had usually entertained enough people to have two tables once a month. The dining table would be laden with goodies from the bakery. The bridge players always killed a bottle of cream sherry in the course of the evening. It was always a convivial affair. With the sherry, it couldn't be otherwise. Deirdre wasn't sure the ladies were great bridge players, but they seemed to roundly enjoy themselves.

Then came the country club set. Again, Deirdre didn't know how often her mother had been in contact with these people. After her father's death, the only people Deirdre was sure her mother kept in touch with regularly were Ginny Finch and Stephanie Lewis. She assumed, though, there were many more. Deirdre had not been that aware of her mother's regular activities.

The garden club was there in full force. It was not particularly unusual for these groups to stick together in these somewhat uncomfortable social situations. She wondered if her mother had had any contact with most of them since her father's death. She doubted it. But they were loyal. She found herself thinking, *Gardeners are like that.*

These clumps of people were followed by many of her friends' mothers and fathers – people her parents had gotten to know when Deirdre and her sisters were growing up. Deirdre had the chance to get updates on friends from the distant and not-so-distant past.

Then came Ginny Finch and Stephanie Lewis themselves. Deirdre had the thought that both of them looked older than her mother, not a comforting thought at a funeral. Both of them were close friends and, after their husbands' deaths, constant companions of her mother. Emily had called them "the three musketeers." As the two approached, Deirdre broke into a reluctant grin. They responded in kind.

Stephanie gave Deirdre's hand a squeeze. "There was

so much more that your mother had yet to do. We were planning Thanksgiving in Vermont."

This was a new piece of information for Deirdre. "Really." Deirdre felt like she had been hit by a truck. Hadn't her mother realized the family was having Thanksgiving together? How very like her to ignore family plans and follow her own whims. After a short conversation, Ginny and Stephanie moved on.

Other short, polite conversations with strangers followed. Deirdre noticed various more familiar people stopping to have longer chats with one or another of her sisters. She saw another close neighbor stop to chat with Emily. Kenneth Ritter, Uncle David's law partner, spent a long time with Penelope. He had spent many Christmas afternoons with the family. She saw that he had finished his chat with Penelope and moved on.

When he reached Deirdre he said with a wry smile, "I've missed your visits to the office. How many years has it been since you moved west?" He seemed to be groping for words. Then he shrugged and blurted out, "I know that you and your mother didn't get along, but she loved you very much. It's important that you know that." It was not new information, but it would have been nice to hear it from her mother – nicer still to have seen it in her mother's actions. Kenneth and Deirdre's conversation was brief after that. Neither one of them knew how to continue. Once again, he smiled and moved on, somewhat hesitantly, as if he had more to say.

As people finished the line, they headed to the buffet table. After a bit, Deirdre realized how hungry she was. She began to wonder when she was going to be able to eat too. It was all well and good that these people had come to the service, but it was beginning to seem they had no manners. To pass the time and take her mind off her stomach, she started noticing, and making silent comments to herself about, people's clothing. She was awfully glad she had been able to pull the clothes she'd worn to her father's funeral, two years before, out of her closet for today's service. At least no one could criticize her. Or maybe they had criticized her then and she was still making the same mistakes.

At last it was over. Almost everyone was gone. The family sat down to eat what they had worked so hard to cook the preceding day. *Not bad,* Deirdre thought to herself. *Mother would have been impressed.* She realized that one of these days she was going to have to stop assessing everything in light of her mother's potential reaction, but not right now.

It was time to thank the crew that had worked so hard with the food and all the associated arrangements. They were from the women's auxiliary and had volunteered to take care of refreshments. Deirdre was not sure they had known what they were in for. They probably did. They probably did this at a lot of funerals. After Deirdre expressed heartfelt thanks, the funeral attendees headed back to Emily's. Tomorrow they would have dinner with Aunt Miriam and Uncle David. The will would be read after the meal. The work of sorting things out would begin in earnest on Monday. The day had been an emotional challenge, even for Deirdre, but the real work lay ahead.

Two

Sunday Dinner

Sunday dinner with Aunt Miriam and Uncle David was a commonplace event throughout the years when the girls were growing up. It was always a treat for them. It had also been a great relief to their mother. To Claire, any dinner preparation was a chore. She had made that abundantly clear. In contrast, for Miriam, every dinner was an adventure.

Those Sunday dinners opened up the world to the girls. Long before they were old enough to venture outside the country, their palates had already traveled the world. Cuisine was a marvelous introduction to culture. Curries, ragouts, risotto – they all held the promise of exciting new worlds. As she grew up, each girl had the double benefit of learning how other peoples lived and how to cook their cuisine, neither of which they would have learned from their mother.

Once Deirdre and her sisters had started to travel, each one had learned as much as she could about her destination before setting out on the trip – making sure, in addition, that she was going to a place where interesting food would be waiting. Deirdre was the first one out of the country. Lured by pasta and sauces, and of course art, she spent her junior year of college abroad in Florence, returning with amazing experiences, a fervent passion for art ... and fifteen pounds heavier.

After the year in Florence, Deirdre met David and Miriam in Zurich. She chose Switzerland because she had spent much time in that country during her year in northern Italy. She had mostly been in the Italian part of Switzerland, the part that is readily accessible from Florence. The German and French parts, though not entirely unknown, remained largely a mystery. With her aunt and uncle, she spent a month traveling in Switzerland. They were merely tourists, vagabonds, staying in family-like settings and really getting to know their hosts and the Swiss customs. In the process, Deirdre and Miriam had been intrigued by, and spent time collecting, Hummel figurines, an occupation that turned out to be lucrative in addition to being satisfying. The value of those little figures shot up in price in only a short time. But the real value of the trip lay in the sights of the Alps and high pastures and in meeting the unpretentious people who lived simple, uncomplicated lives amid that breathtaking scenery.

For months after they'd returned home, Miriam had served meals that reminded Deirdre of that carefree interlude. Deirdre took home with her the knowledge of how to prepare simple but tasty peasant meals. Deirdre's favorite was cheese fondue. Most useful was the knowledge that only six ingredients were needed to turn out a respectable fondue.

Miriam and David learned much about foreign foods in their extensive travels. As they traveled, Miriam learned a lot about the cooking. David learned much about the eating. But they were not just gourmets. Their home was also filled with the reminders of their adventures. Better than merely souvenirs, these items represented happy memories. Some were actually fairly valuable. They came home from a vacation in Austria with an antique music box that played the opening bars of a Mozart symphony. Of greater interest to their nieces were the Mozart candies they brought back, those delectable balls of marzipan wrapped in chocolate. Their taste would stay on Deirdre's tongue forever.

The vacation in Switzerland was the culmination of many years of preparation and anticipation. When Deirdre was just ten, her parents took a trip to Europe. In retrospect, Deirdre realized that her mother had been thinking about another baby. The trip had been her father's way of buying Claire off, of keeping the family size manageable. At the time, Penelope was three, not quite as charming a little girl as she once was. Penelope was beginning to have her own thoughts and desires and was just starting to have little disagreements with her mother. Funny how that worked. The girls' personalities were their own. Once children left the adorable and innocent stage, it was time for another – at least in Claire's world.

During that time, while the parents were away, Miriam and David had stayed with the four girls. It was a three-week delight for all of them. While never quite being ready to be parents, David and Miriam were ready to act as surrogates … as long as they didn't have to do it for long. For those three weeks, curfews, while not entirely abandoned, were put on the back burner. And while the girls and their stand-in parents were not traveling, they all ate like they were.

After that episode, Deirdre started stopping in at Miriam and David's house on her way home from school. She received another early taste of the promise of world travel and learned to nurture it during those visits. She and Miriam started playing double solitaire. They "bought" their decks of cards for fifty-two dollars each. For every card up, they got five dollars back. At the end of every game, they counted their winnings. At the end of an afternoon, they would tally up the total and plan extravagant trips to every corner of the globe. Then Deirdre had her homework cut out for her. She would research the country, not only for cuisine but for history, customs, and anything else appropriate. If it seemed a likely candidate for a visit, that country would then find its way onto her list. So while all four sisters had a lengthy history with their aunt and uncle, Deirdre's affinity for them was particularly strong.

That Sunday, the day following the funeral, Deirdre and Penelope arrived early at David and Miriam's home to enable them to spend as much time as possible with Aunt Miriam. They quickly resumed their roles as sous-chefs and got to work peeling potatoes, making piecrusts, and whipping cream. Rather than making an exotic menu,

Miriam had planned a traditional New England dinner. It was harvest time, and it was too tempting for her not to use the fresh ingredients at hand. Taking a cue from his brother-in-law, David had long since become an avid vegetable gardener. His vegetable garden was now almost fifty square feet. Most of the vegetables for the dinner were ones that he had grown.

In her youth, Deirdre had spent as much time with her uncle in his vegetable garden as she'd spent in her father's garden at home. Because of those early days, she almost felt an ownership of the food that they would have for dinner that evening. She had yet to develop an understanding of vegetable gardening in the Northwest, a fact that never ceased to dismay her. The climate was too different and, to Deirdre, too arbitrary. When she discovered that the easy-to-grow tomato was next to impossible to grow there, she reluctantly gave up trying. The lack of sun in the Northwest was just too daunting.

Before Deirdre could get worked up again about her inability to grow vegetables in her current home, Caroline and Emily arrived. They enthusiastically pitched in with the meal preparation. But there is an awful lot of truth to the saying that too many cooks spoil the broth. Miriam wasn't about to see her meal ruined. Deirdre knew that Miriam had that saying in mind when she relieved her two older nieces of their duties. Miriam did, however, continue to supervise the kitchen activities – in a halfhearted way. She mostly diverted her attention to Emily and Deirdre, knowing that Caroline and Penelope were entirely capable of turning out the meal without supervision.

When the dinner preparation was well underway,

Kenneth Ritter arrived. Kenneth was not only David's law partner, he was also one of Miriam and David's closest friends. His presence harkened back to those early Sunday dinners. Kenneth was a bachelor and often had joined the family for meals on the weekend. It seemed totally natural that he would be there now.

After the meal went in the oven, they sat down over cups of passion fruit tea, a discovery that Deirdre had made on a recent trip to Hawaii. It was a novelty to everyone and a taste sensation. Deirdre felt smug when she introduced the tea to the rest of the family. Their reactions were as rewarding as she had hoped. While the whole ensemble was waiting for the meal to cook, they touched on foreign affairs, travel, and cooking. Dinner itself was ready far earlier than anyone expected. The group simply moved the action and conversation along with the food to the dining room. Everyone marveled that so many years had passed since those early dinners together. Again they dismissed the idea the years could possibly show.

Miriam and David had marvelous senses of humor, both mischievous and black. The added years did not affect that humor. Aging had only fine-tuned it and softened its edges. Their adventurous spirit and lightheartedness helped lift some of the gravity of the recent events. The loss of a younger sister, while sorrowful, was not something that David could not overcome with time. Miriam had suffered her own losses, long ago, and had put them far behind. Her eyes had regained and now kept their infectious twinkle. She bore little evidence of the years she had lived, something that irritated her friends no end.

David was little different. He was a short and muscular man, blond and robust, in a way that Deirdre had always admired. Deirdre looked more like her mother and her uncle, while her sisters were all unmistakably Lincolns. Because Miriam and David did not have children, they were, to Deirdre, more like coconspirators than parents. Deirdre had always been her aunt and uncle's favorite, something she had relished but never quite understood. It seemed to her then, as it did now, that there was, inexplicably, no age difference between them.

Dinner was lovely and convivial, a delightful harvest feast. The conversation focused on what the sisters were doing in their respective lives. Once in a while they would discuss politics or the abstract points of law involved in one of the cases that David or Kenneth was working on. Even though it was hardly a mystery why they were together, Claire hardly had a presence in the conversation. At the end of the main course, they broke with tradition and ate dessert at the dinner table rather than in the living room, hurrying a bit so that the business they had gathered to attend to could get started. In the relaxed tradition of past Sunday dinners, they took their tea into the living room.

Once ensconced in the living room with the pot of tea, the group lingered with their cups rather than turning their attention to the will. Each of the four daughters was reluctant to read the document they suspected would lead to the dissolution of their connection to the house all their earliest memories were tied to. They were all more than aware that their mother was gone, but none of them was ready to further sever their links to the past. As they sipped their after-dinner beverage, they also drank in the rustic but elegant charm that Miriam had created in her home. While David had been busy with his law practice, she had devoted herself to, among many other things, making her home a comfortable place to live and entertain guests.

While Deirdre was contemplating the extent of their loss with part of her mind, another part was diverted by her taste buds. She silently complimented Miriam on the exquisite maple mousse. What a perfect dessert for a harvest meal! She also found herself marveling over how the tea that Miriam had selected complemented the autumn flavors so well. Miriam was a genius at blending tastes, something that Deirdre, with all her experience at gardening and working with natural ingredients, still found elusive.

Deirdre poured herself another cup of tea and pondered her sisters' relationships to their hometown now that their mother was no longer alive. Far too many places existed in town that Emily would have to avoid in the coming months, places that Emily and her mother had frequented together. She wondered how often Caroline would return to the old stomping grounds. It was fairly clear to her that wasn't a concern for Penelope. To Deirdre's way of thinking, Penelope's future visits to the town would be as infrequent as her own. With all these factors, the place where she had grown up would always hold a special place in her heart.

It seemed so much easier to everyone sitting around the living room to linger and continue the casual conversation from dinner rather than darken the mood by dealing with the will. But, they couldn't put it off forever. Sooner or later, they were going to have to begin, so Uncle David finally decided it was time to turn attention to the serious matters that shouldn't be avoided much longer.

David Solstrand was his sister's executor. He had also, in his capacity as her lawyer, been privy to her affairs and drawn up the will. Therefore, he knew its contents. This would be the first time, though, that any of her girls would know the terms of their mother's will. Deirdre agreed with David's estimation that the easiest way to approach the whole matter was just to start reading the document. "I, Claire Lincoln, being of sound mind and body ..."

Boy, that's a stretch. Deirdre did not quite dare share her thoughts, but she wondered which of her sisters was thinking the same thing. David wondered too. He was not unaware of the distance between his sister and her three younger daughters. Silent skepticism hung heavily in the room. He paused and looked up, deciding that a different approach would make more sense.

"I'm going to dispense with reading the document and just give you the gist. As you know, I'm the executor. I will have my firm make you copies of the will. I'll bring them home tomorrow night. If you want to stop by the office to pick a copy up before that, it will be there waiting for you." He continued with the summary. "You will all inherit the house in equal portions. Aside from specific bequests, the same is true of the contents. I want you all to decide how the contents are going to be divided. Each of you will get one of the Oriental rugs. Decide among yourselves who gets which. I'm leaving you all a lot of discretion. I know that you are all up to it, won't disappoint me, and won't overstep the bounds of fairness.

"Your father was prudent with his investments. Your mother never veered from what he had done. I have been your mother's financial advisor for the past two years. The four of you also will get the portfolio and liquid assets in equal portions. The only thing that will not be equal is the distribution of your mother's considerable wardrobe. I know we all joked for years about Deirdre being the runt of the litter, but she is the only one small enough to wear any of your mother's clothing."

Although this was not news to any of them, Emily, Caroline, and Penelope felt the loss keenly because their mother really was quite a clotheshorse. Deirdre jumped in, trying to ease the disappointment as best she could. "I think that all the scarves, purses, and other items that are not related to size go into the pot for us all to split. But don't think that there are not items in those categories that I won't fight for. Just so you know." Deirdre's smile was broad and innocent.

David continued, "You will all also split your mother's jewelry, although Deirdre ought to get less because of her good fortune with the wardrobe. There are specific jewelry bequests; your mother left her diamond engagement ring to you, Emily. Deirdre, you will get your mother's aquamarine ring. It was her birthstone and, as you all know, she never took it off. The funeral home gave both rings to me, and I put them in her jewelry box."

"Aren't we lucky they were so conscientious?" Caroline showed her relief.

David picked up where he left off. "Caroline, you're next. You're lucky that you're a Libra. You'll get the opal ring and also that outstanding opal watch. That leaves you, Penelope. The pearl ring is yours – another birthstone. I know this is none of my business, but I think Penelope should have that great pearl necklace to wear when the orchestra is playing."

Penelope beamed and, of course, agreed. It didn't show, but the whole process was actually much more stressful than any of them had anticipated.

David went on. "There is one more jewelry bequest. Your mother left the necklace with the butterfly inside of it to Deirdre. Em, you're going to have to rearrange your living room. Molly hit the jackpot. Your mother was impressed by her attention to her music. Now, she'll have to get even more serious. To make sure that her progress continues, Molly is getting the baby grand piano. I think tomorrow you should all go over together and map out a plan for going through the house's contents. After a short time, we will want to put the house on the market. In the meantime, we are lucky that Deirdre will be here until after Thanksgiving. Deirdre, you have your work cut out for you. It's not going to be easy, but I know you have it in you. With any luck, the house will sell before you leave. Wouldn't that be nice? Another small detail – you have to consider what to do with Solomon. Is he going to stay at Emily's?"

Claire had been passionate about cats. Solomon was only four, a mere youngster. The girls had grown up with cats. It was unusual, surprisingly so, that there was no cat in Emily's household. But, luckily, particularly for Solomon, he was welcomed there now.

Deirdre quickly jumped in. "I think I would like to have Solomon's company for the next two months. It's his house, and he should be presented with just one change at a time. Besides, I like Solomon."

Emily agreed once again that they would love to have him at their house permanently when Deirdre was ready for him to leave Round Hill Road. The kids were so fond of him.

Having dealt with the preliminary details, David especially was happy to leave the will behind. They got back to spending a pleasant evening reminiscing about evenings past. They started planning out how to attack the house but decided they would figure that out in the days to come. They would start the following day, but Emily, Caroline, and Penelope hoped that Deirdre would do the bulk of the work.

At that point, they switched to travel plans. It seemed only natural, given their reluctance to meet the real reason for their gathering head-on. For Emily, travel meant summer vacations that were children-friendly. The legacy would enable Emily and Tom to buy a timeshare at Disneyland. For the rest of them, the legacy gave them new travel possibilities – Europe and maybe even South America. Deirdre felt abashed that she was even thinking about travel plans at this time. But she was. And she knew that at least Miriam would also be on that wavelength. The inheritance also made possible the plans that had been incubating in Deirdre and Jeremy's minds. They wanted to expand the nursery. The infusion of capital into their coffers would be very timely.

In the midst of all this family discussion, Kenneth looked a little bit out of his element, although not awkward or embarrassed, as some in his place might be.

The interpersonal dynamics at work here were ones that Kenneth, as almost family, was certain to understand. Deirdre was comfortable with him being present. The family had known him forever and he had to be grieving too.

It struck Deirdre that because Kenneth had handled so many wills, he would not find any of their reactions atypical. They were fairly common in most ways. Kenneth was familiar enough with each of the girls to know none of them would squander their good fortunes but, rather, would use them wisely. It was more than likely that he was pleased with what he was sensing. Deirdre knew that looking at the whole situation from an outsider's perspective one would realize that tangible matters are one thing, emotional ones entirely different. Kenneth was not, however, an outsider.

The Old Homestead

The funeral was over. The will had been read. All of Claire's daughters had a lifetime to deal with the emotional aftermath of the loss of their mother but only a limited amount of time to empty the house of the contents that had been amassed in their youths and beyond. So much of their early lives were tied up with that house. If they didn't uncover some of those memories now, they never would. Because David suggested it and because Caroline and Penelope were only going to be in town for a week, the sisters decided to get right to work on Monday morning.

Deirdre and Penelope drove over to the house on Round Hill Road in Penelope's car, while Caroline and Emily stayed behind to get the kids off to school. Looking at the car, Deirdre wondered how on earth Penelope had made it all the way from Hartford. The car had obviously been used when Penelope bought it, and she had put at least fifty thousand miles on it since then. And what was really under the hood? The paint was faded, and the upholstery had places where the stuffing was poking out. Turning to her sister, Deirdre said, "We still need Caroline's concurrence, but Emily and I think you should replace this old crate with Mother's car. What do you think?"

Penelope was quick to answer. "My car is so decrepit there is always the question of arriving anywhere. But this is a week too late. Last week, I took a look at my finances, took a deep breath, and ordered a new car. Besides, her car is too fancy for me." The upholstery was of the highest quality, and the car even had seat heat. Its sound system was something Derek would have approved of but never paid for.

Deirdre sighed audibly. She wasn't surprised by Penelope's response. "I'm sorry to hear that. But, you're right. Mother never let cost get in the way when she wanted something. I think that such a high-end car will be more up Caroline's alley anyway."

Penelope looked abashed that she was refusing such an offer. She gave Deirdre a quizzical look. "I can't fit everything in this car, though, and multiple trips might kill it. It's got to be running so I can trade it in."

"Well, Tom is having a trailer hitch put on Mother's car this week. He is going to drive Caroline down to DC next weekend with a trailer and then drive back the following day. After that, I'm going to need the car as long as I'm in the east. The last thing I want is to be stuck without a car and dependent on Emily for transportation. You can use Mother's car to take all your stuff back to Hartford as long as you leave me your car in its place."

Deirdre paused briefly with a horrified look on her face. "What am I saying? I guess I'll have to take my chances with your car. But only for a day. Anyway, keep the possibility of using the car with the trailer in mind."

Marginal as it was, Penelope's car once again reached its destination and delivered its occupants to their goal. When Deirdre and Penelope pulled up to the house, they saw that the foliage of the big old maple was starting to turn a luminescent crimson. In another week, its leaves would be as vibrant as it had been in its best years. Actually, Deirdre could not remember a year when it had not performed spectacularly – at least in all the years she'd lived there. In the recesses of her mind, she could picture herself playing under that tree with the son of one of her mother's friends. She had not much liked the boy, but she remembered enjoying the day. It was a great tree to play under. Her memories were as rosy as the autumn leaves. Her mother had had the habit of foisting her friends' children on her own. The girls had actually made some good friends, and had tolerated others. At least none had been so objectionable as to ruin a day's play.

They parked in front of the garage and headed to the back door. When Deirdre had been a teenager, she had hated coming home. She had looked forward to the day when she would not have to live there anymore. Now, she was looking with a pang to the time when the house would be sold and no longer in the family. There was, however, a lot of work to be done before that time.

As they walked toward the back door, Penelope was in front of her. Deirdre looked at her sister with amazement that the little girl she remembered had grown into such a remarkable young woman, regretting the years she had missed of Penelope's young life. At the same time, she knew she would have been fighting with her mother had she lived nearby. Her high school years were fraught with anxiety and more than a little tension. Those years had passed in a state of armed truce. She was wise never to have returned to North Linton or, as she preferred to think of it, the scene of the crime.

The back door opened onto the kitchen. The room was both familiar and strange at the same time. Deirdre felt reassured by the sight of the white, painted cabinets. The cabinets even looked like they had been recently cleaned. That was certainly a novelty. After a brief period of looking around and silently remembering both happy and turbulent times, Deirdre suggested a starting place. "Since we'll all be staying here, we should make a shopping list." Penelope set about opening cupboards, ready to take stock of the food supply. Deirdre was surprised that her mother's larder was so well stocked. "It looks as though Mother has been eating very well."

"Her housekeeper, Josephine, cooked all her meals. Believe me, she's a better cook than any of us ever was." Penelope looked like she was not yet over the fact that anyone could make a better meal in the Lincoln kitchen than a Lincoln.

For the time being, Deirdre and her sisters would have to buy less than originally thought. Emily had let Deirdre know she'd told Josephine to take anything that would go bad from the refrigerator and that she was welcome to anything else. What remained were just staples.

They spent a good hour making a temporary list, a

list of foods that would get them through for a week or ten days. Their shopping would be particularly important because they had such different eating habits. Penelope followed a health-food regimen; Deirdre ate very little meat; Caroline was a gourmet. Deirdre knew it would be a challenge to concoct meals that satisfied them all.

As Deirdre finished the list and closed the pantry Penelope wandered into the dining room. All the favorite family dishes, glasses, and other tableware were in that room. The sisters would have to divide those valued items. Deirdre and Penelope had both decided that day was as good a time as any to discuss the dining room contents. When Deirdre joined Penelope she saw the linen already out of the cupboard and arrayed on the table. Her eyes lighted up at the sight of the mint green tablecloth.

"Looks like Christmas to me. Penelope, can you recall a single Christmas we didn't use that green cloth?"

Grinning, Penelope answered "I have a vivid picture of those Christmas dinners. It was years before I realized that most people have roast turkey at Christmas." She blushed at her naïveté. "It still seems wrong. That's Thanksgiving food. Roast beef and Yorkshire pudding are the normal Christmas food."

Deirdre broke in, "Food aside, I remember the year that Grandma and Grandpa Lincoln came over for dinner with Uncle David, Aunt Miriam, and Kenneth Ritter. That was the year we all got those wonderful red, quilted satin bathrobes that Grandma Lincoln made."

Penelope looked as if she still couldn't quite understand why her closet no longer has a red, satin bathrobe. "Being the youngest I wore those bathrobes, one after another, for twelve years. Kenneth gave us Chinese satin slippers that year too. Do you remember them? It broke my heart when I outgrew the last bathrobe and set of matching slippers." Deirdre smiled warmly. "That was the year Grandpa Lincoln sang the Whiffenpoof song for you. You cried about little lost lambs for days after that."

Penelope had a wistful look on her face. "I still can't hear that song without at least feeling sad. Sometimes I do mist over."

It seemed that memories would continually get in the way of their cleaning. They knew, though, they would never have another chance to call up these memories so vividly. It was going to be a week of reliving a lot of their past.

Before Emily and Caroline arrived, Deirdre and Penelope went into the living room and pulled more visions from the past out of the air. "And there was the Christmas that Daddy and Mother gave me my first flute." Penelope was radiant. "Little did they know where that would lead."

Deirdre added her only clear vision of that holiday. "That was the year the rest of us got a lot of classical music. Daddy always made sure that the presents we got were ones he already had or would want for himself."

They lingered in the living room, sinking into the plush sofa as if the intervening years had never happened. Penelope felt that it was the right time to bring up a topic she had long wanted to talk to Deirdre about. "Jon will come up with Caroline for Thanksgiving. Jeremy will fly out to join you. This is going to be a real family time. Do you think Emily will mind if I bring Nora?"

Deirdre paused before answering. The issue of her sister's sexuality had first arisen in her mind a few years earlier but had remained a question. "I think that would be just fine. I think you are sharing something long overdue with me. Am I right?" She was not sure that she was using the right words. But she was glad that her sister was finally trusting her with this information. Letting Penelope continue in her own words, Deirdre remained silent.

"This is not something I was comfortable talking about when Mother was alive." Penelope spoke awkwardly. "Obviously I would prefer that this coronary never happened. I would have found a way to cope with her criticism sooner or later. She always thought I didn't have boyfriends because I had a personality problem. In her eyes, it was something that was all my fault. No need to put it off much longer now. It is a trade-off I would rather not have had to make. But now I can at least be me."

Hoping that she sounded appropriately welcoming and wanting to keep the conversation open, Deirdre responded, "I think Thanksgiving would be a delightful time to get to know Nora." She knew this was just the beginning of many talks she and Penelope would have on the subject. "I don't want to pry. Tell me as much or as little about Nora as you want."

"I'll let you form your opinion by meeting her. She is someone I met at the orchestra, so she can't be all bad. She plays cello."

"Now I can see why you had your own issues with Mother. I thought maybe I was the only one." Deirdre added in an envious voice, "I love tenor instruments. You've got yourself a good start for a chamber orchestra."

First Steps

At that point, Emily and Caroline arrived. They looked ready for the day's work. Emily, dressed in clothes she usually wore when she worked in her garden, was jaunty and had shed her matronly appearance. To Deirdre, she looked ten years younger. Caroline was wearing the same tailored blue jeans she had worn the day before the funeral, but, in recognition of the work that faced them, she had borrowed an old sweater from Emily. It seemed likely to Deirdre that Caroline would have preferred something more stylish, but Emily had decided a work session didn't call for style.

After greeting them, Deirdre switched topics. "I know that we've been here a while, but we were just getting started when we got distracted with reliving past moments, holidays and stuff."

Emily was peevish. "I would have thought you'd have gotten something done by now."

Deirdre jumped to her own defense. "We did make

a grocery list that should take us through the week. Penelope and I will go shopping when we're done here." She continued by outlining her thoughts about the approach they should take toward the house and its contents. "I would like to act as the foreman for the whole process of dismantling the household. It makes sense to me that I be the one to direct things since I'll be staying in the house for the next two months. I think we should aim for November first to put the house on the market."

Caroline looked relieved. "I was wondering how we were going to do this. It all seems so ghoulish. I know we can be accused of being scavengers. I would prefer to think of it as salvaging parts of our past. So where do we start?"

Deirdre answered, "We should go through as much of the downstairs as we can while you two are still here. Today, I would like to make some decisions about the large pieces of furniture. Before any of us takes anything, we should all concur, unless, of course it's in the will. Agreed?"

Everyone agreed. Caroline was hesitant about her wants but, after a short interval, ventured her thoughts: "The only thing that I can imagine fitting in with my furniture is the dry bar. None of this colonial stuff. I do think that I would like to throw my Oriental rug back into the mix. Would you all consider letting me have Mother's car instead?"

"Deirdre and I were talking about that earlier." Penelope was pleased that the car's disposition would be so easy.

Deirdre cast a knowing glance in her direction. "Sounds good to me. Em, looks like the furniture division is between the three of us. I can't imagine dragging a lot of stuff across the country, but I would like a few small early American pieces. You cannot, for obvious reasons, find them out there – at any price. I would also like the secretary. I'll bargain. This is not hard and fast. I'm willing to let Penelope have most of my share."

"Our house can't absorb much. We're going to have to do some major rearranging to make room for Molly's piano." Emily was pensive. She looked as though she was not pleased at the coming disruption to her household. That displeasure vanished as she found further advantages for her children. "I think the sea chest will fit in Ben's room and will be a good toy box for him. Solomon's chair will easily fit in Bonnie's room. Won't she be pleased? Other than that, I can't picture anything else fitting. And yes, Caroline is welcome to Mother's car."

Deirdre threw in a request that had been in the back of her mind, "Jeremy and I have been considering adding music to the nursery. I know this is not in the large furniture category, but I would like Daddy's sound system. May I?"

The gardener in Caroline was green with envy. "You'd have a hard time keeping me away from a nursery like that. Beauty for the senses. Yours is not a job. It's a way of life one can only wish for."

That seemed to cover the large furniture division for the time being. There would, doubtless, be fine-tuning, but they were satisfied that they had made as much progress as they could without further time passing. And so Deirdre headed upstairs, leaving her sisters to work in the dining room.

Deirdre was startled when she reached the second-floor landing. What had happened to the upstairs since she had last been there took her by surprise. One of the bedrooms had been transformed into a small office. Another was a full-fledged guestroom, a luxury that, with four daughters, her parents had never had. The small room leading into her parents' bedroom, which had housed her father's bureau and had been his dressing room, was now her mother's sitting room. Two years after his death, no sign of her father ever having lived in the house remained. The entire color scheme of the master bedroom had changed. Her father never would have put up with the soft blue and rose tones that now defined the room. It was too feminine. There were some new pieces of furniture as well. It was definitely a woman's room.

To Deirdre, the room had always been her parents' bedroom, the room to which she and her sisters had taken their stockings on Christmas morning, the room they had gone to for comfort on one of the manifold occasions of childhood distress, the room they crept into late at night when they had exciting news to report or simply to let their parents know that they had returned home safely. Her other sisters had probably gotten used to the changes, but they hit Deirdre in the face. The bedroom had always reflected both her parents' personalities. She knew she had to get used to the changes. Actually, she didn't. The house would soon have new owners, and it would no longer be her concern.

Unable to mentally process the changes right away, Deirdre rejoined her sisters, who were starting to box up a lot of the dining room dishes. "What on earth did

Mother do up there? I would never recognize it as the place I grew up."

Emily said, "It was hard to get used to at first, but I guess it's something that's old hat after only a year."

The momentary awkwardness dampened any further comment. Emily, Caroline, and Penelope returned to packing the dishes, leaving Deirdre to come to terms with the changes she had just encountered. Since Penelope didn't have enough dishes to serve a dinner for eight, those boxes were destined for her. Once the dishes were wrapped up, they moved on to other, incidental dining room items. The four of them decided to put off going to the supermarket until the following day, rather than shopping for food before they had some solid accomplishments, and food, under their belts. They continued with the work they were doing, just more slowly.

By the end of the afternoon, they were all exhausted, a hint of what the next two months held, particularly for Deirdre. Emily was the first one to peter out, soon followed by all three of her sisters. A "kickoff" dinner was in order before the real work began.

While they enjoyed a quiet meal at a favorite local restaurant, the four discussed how their new status as orphans affected them. For Penelope, it meant sharing parts of herself that had remained hidden for years. She had started to reveal those hidden parts to Deirdre. Now she found that it felt good to have the floodgates open to her other sisters too. Caroline and Emily were more nonplussed than Deirdre had been. Unlike Deirdre, they had had no suspicions. Penelope was truly saddened by her mother's death but glad that she could finally open up to her family. A huge weight had been finally lifted. "Mother would have hated me if she had known." Penelope wore a rueful expression.

Caroline was quick to express her empathy. "I'm so sorry you had to wait this long to tell us. Of course we would love to meet Nora."

The sisters' emotions seemed to range on a sliding scale. For Emily, the fact of her mother's death would be something to be reckoned with for a long time. In a sense, Emily had relied on her mother for the things her mother did as a grandmother – caring, doting, and attention giving. Emily had also relied on her mother for advice on her weekly column. Her mother had been a quite honest critic. Most mothers find it hard to say anything critical; Claire never had that problem. Emily knew, though, that the severity of her feelings would be short-lived.

For her part, Deirdre admitted that she lived too far away to be much affected. "If you didn't suspect it, I moved west in large part to get away from Mother. The move, in some ways, only served to make something that already existed more tangible." None of them was surprised.

Caroline had mixed emotions. "I didn't expect this would have such a big impact on me. We drifted further apart after Daddy died. Mother thought we'd end up closer. I also know the pangs won't last terribly long." What was noteworthy was that all four of them were having the kind of discussion that they never had before. They had always guessed how each other felt but never actually vocalized their thoughts to each other.

Deirdre brought the conversation back to the work that needed to be done. "While the weather is still nice, I'm going to clean up the yard. I can't believe how Mother has let it go to pot since Daddy died. I'm going to get out there early tomorrow morning."

After the dinner, Emily got ready to go back to her house. "Good luck deciding where you're all going to sleep. After today's work session, you probably want nothing better than to give your weary bodies some welcome rest. I know I do."

Once they arrived back at the house, Deirdre and her two younger sisters found the decision of where to sleep harder than they originally thought. Their mother had muddied things when she'd created the small study. Deirdre ended up sleeping in the room that had been her bedroom after Emily had gone to college. Caroline and Penelope stayed in the bedroom they had shared for most of their youth.

The bedrooms in the Lincoln home had undergone continual changes in "ownership" over the years. The room their mother had converted to a study was what they had always called the "baby room." Each of them had started out in that room. As soon as the next baby was close to arriving, there was an occupant/bedroom shuffle. Deirdre had moved in with Emily when Caroline was due and about to become the new baby room occupant. When Penelope had arrived, Emily had moved into what would never again be the guest room and Caroline had become Deirdre's new roommate. When Deirdre finally figured out that it was not fair for Penelope to have a room of her own while she was still stuck with Caroline, a new move was engineered. Penelope became Caroline's new roommate and the baby room was, once again, Deirdre's room. Then when Emily went to college, Deirdre moved into Emily's bedroom, at which point Penelope moved back to the baby room.

The bedroom that had started as the guest room and finished as Deirdre's room had the best view on the property. Just outside was the oldest and most magnificent tree. It wasn't actually close, but it was so big it couldn't be any closer. It was a big old maple that, in the fall, turned a lit-from-within red. Deirdre had never seen the display equaled. She had spent so much time relating to that tree one could almost call it communing. As a little girl, Deirdre had played under that tree in spring and summer. She'd watched the leaves turn red and then fall in autumn, raking them into a big pile and jumping into it delightedly. She'd seen the snow accumulate on its bare branches. Her heart had warmed as the icicles had started to drip and the first robin of the season had come to perch on its limbs, announcing spring. What a treat that she would be there to see it in its glory once again.

Now, as Deirdre settled into the room, Caroline came in, lingering, pensively. Penelope was in the room that she and Caroline would share, but Caroline wanted to talk to Deirdre a little more about the happenings of the past week. "This is an obvious thing to say. I will miss her. I've never been an orphan before."

Deirdre jumped in quickly. "Oh, don't get me wrong. I will miss her too. You may not realize this, but I have great memories. It's just that I had major issues as well."

Caroline continued where she had left off as soon as Deirdre stopped talking. "Mother taught me, among other things, how to be a lady. When I started to grow bigger than her, she convinced me it was okay. I was worried I was going to be this big, awkward girl, but she told me about tall and slim, elegant women. Got me over a big hurdle. But that was her main contribution to my adolescence. I never felt that she had any idea who I really was. Did she guide you through your adolescence and then figure you would help me?"

Deirdre reflected briefly. "No. She left that job to Emily. You'll have to ask Emily if she got the original help and was expected to pass it on. I imagine she left that to Daddy. I wished so much for Mother to give me the kind of quick fix she apparently gave you about your looks. But even that was not to happen while I was still living at home. I learned more from Daddy – not just facts, although I did learn a lot of those. I got a passion for reading, I guess from both Daddy and Mother. But I got the ability to evaluate people and events critically from Daddy. Mother's biggest contribution there was to step back and try not to interfere. She wasn't bad at leaving us to our own devices, was she? Having said that, I'll stop talking. I'm not extremely tired, but we have a long day ahead of us – no, make that a long week."

Caroline was quick to agree. "I think I'll turn in but spend a little time chatting with Penelope first. It's wonderful to be here with all of you and with the big maple putting on its annual show. Good night. Parting is such sweet sorrow … But we'll still be together tomorrow."

OUT IN THE GARDEN

It was bright blue and balmy that Tuesday morning. Regardless of where in the country she was, Deirdre woke up as soon as it was light. Her circadian rhythms were closely tied to the sun. It doubtless came from being a gardener. It was getting close to autumn, but there was no other phrase to describe this beautiful day but *Indian summer.* Such warm weather so late in the year was almost like borrowed time. It was not to be wasted. As a native New Englander, she knew from experience that the temperature could drop without warning.

The garden needed to be cleaned up before it was too late to consider doing so. This would be the perfect day to do that. Deirdre wanted to work in the yard so the house would look better for selling. This would also be the last time to see the garden she had grown up with. She considered going outside before breakfast but then realized she would have more staying power if she ate first. Although she didn't delay in getting to the kitchen,

Solomon beat her there. She fed him and then made herself a hearty drink of milk, fruit, and honey.

There was no sign yet of either one of her sisters. They had all planned to go shopping for the week's food right after breakfast, but the warm weather was just too nice to pass up. The outdoors beckoned. Deirdre left a note for Caroline and Penelope in case they had forgotten her words from the previous evening. Then she headed outside to face the weeds. "C'mon, big fella, you beautiful guy." Once again, Solomon beat her. She turned the doorknob, and he dashed out.

Deirdre was astounded that anyone who belonged to a garden club could put up with such a crop of weeds. Her mother had been a fairly decent gardener before her father had died. Her parents had worked together to keep the yard a showplace. Apparently, it was not work her mother had been terribly serious about. Now it certainly looked like Claire had abandoned any effort to maintain the gardens. After Derek's death, Claire had engaged a lawn service. But that was all the workers did. Just the lawn. They obviously did not pay any attention to the flower beds. But even the lawn had those charming weeds that no one in the country seems able to avoid, those lion's teeth or dandelions.

Deirdre was constantly surprised at how much she missed getting dirt under her fingernails. She classified herself as one of the addicted gardeners their business catered to. Only a week had passed since she had worked in a garden, but it felt terrific to get her hands back in the soil after only a short time away. She looked, with dismay, at all the flower beds. The yard had been her father's pride and joy. The many years she had spent outside with him came flooding back. She had gotten her first lessons about the many classes of plants and how they related to the variety in human nature in those sessions outdoors. She had learned so much about both horticulture and humanity under her father's tutelage.

Her first gardening experience had been growing vegetables when she was eight years old. Her father had started her out with radishes because it only takes four weeks from seed to mature vegetable. It was a great way to introduce a little girl to the wonders of growing food. They had also grown tomatoes and pole beans that first year. It was then that Deirdre had learned the first lesson about plants – there are plants that nourish your body.

That was the same year her father introduced her to flowering annuals – marigolds, petunias, and zinnias. Annuals don't need a lot of care, just some water and attention at the beginning. Such paltry efforts rewarded her with continuous bloom for the season. They were, in one sense, just another food plant. The food they provided just nourished a different part of the body. This was food for the soul.

Annuals are infinitely more colorful and, in that way, more rewarding, but they are disappointingly different in that they are exactly what their name says – annual. When the frost comes, the gardener is in the same boat as at the start. The following year, one has to start all over from scratch. It is an evanescent beauty, but beauty nonetheless. This was one of Deirdre's first lessons. Annuals are, in that sense, fickle and inconstant – not the attributes one would look for in a friend either.

It was in that first gardening year that she had discovered the garden as the perfect place to play. She had let her imagination run free and realized that the plants were just like toys – versatile and ready to be turned into whatever she wanted. One day, the hollyhocks were young women dressed up for a dance. The next day, the rose bugs were the material for the budding scientist to use in her laboratory. Another day, she was the head warden, and the marigolds her sentinels in the fight against those bright green criminals, the tomato worms. When the cold weather came and stopped her outdoor activities, Deirdre learned to bury herself in seed catalogs.

Those days were far in the past. Continuing her cleanup effort, she moved on to the perennial beds. The true champions, in the garden and in life, are the hardy perennials. They require thought and consideration at the outset. After that, they are faithful companions unless one does something hideous. This is not to say that they shouldn't always be given thought and consideration. It's just that they're less likely to hold a grudge unless they are neglected for a while. As she had these thoughts, she cast a whimsical look at the old, gnarled maple tree. While not a plant, it had the same characteristics as a perennial. It dropped its leaves at the end of the growing season and went to sleep for the winter. She had never known whether or not that particular tree was a sugar maple. Its physical beauty made her think that it had the kind of beauty that would appeal to the taste palate as well as the visual one.

Deirdre realized she was letting her emotions from the past get the better of her. She knew she needed to join her sisters for a real breakfast and judged that, for now, the best plan of action would be to limit herself to cleaning up the perennial beds. She would make divisions to give to Emily and Caroline. Perhaps Penelope would like some for her friends. On second thought, after hearing the terms of the will, it seemed likely that Penelope would soon buy a house of her own and would need some landscaping. There were certain plants Deirdre, herself, would love to have for sentimental reasons, but logistics made that next to impossible. Maybe at some point she could get divisions of plants that she gave to Emily. This was not the end of the road for these plants and the Lincoln family.

Approaching the first perennial bed, Deirdre felt her heart sink when she saw the condition of the hollyhocks. They were surrounded by high, grassy weeds, which made those ladies' ball gowns look shabby. How could Deirdre dance with these poor specimens? Her rescue efforts yielded the desired results. Even this late in the season the weeding made a noticeable difference. After she had satisfied herself there was nothing more to be done with the hollyhocks, Deirdre moved on. She had expected to find delphiniums in front of the hollyhocks. Initially puzzled at their absence, she realized, *Of course. Delphiniums are biennials. They would have needed replanting. Daddy wasn't here to do that.* The garden wasn't the same without that heavenly blue. Closing her eyes, she could picture Rudbeckia next to where the delphiniums should have been. Opening them, she saw that her memory wasn't entirely wrong. What was wrong was the condition of the sorry black-eyed-susans. They were inundated with weeds. Luckily, what was left of them could be reclaimed.

An angry chattering broke the morning silence – just in case she needed to be reminded she was back in New England once again. She wasn't sure if she or Solomon was the offender, but one of them had disturbed the local blue jay. In all likelihood, it would be dive-bombing them soon. Looking overhead, she spotted the culprit in the lower branches of a tree twenty feet away. The jay had dismissed Solomon as an opponent that could easily be taken on. It was now eyeing Deirdre as if summing her up. Deirdre found herself thinking of the bird as he. Realizing that was an error that all people commonly make, she then decided that, in this instance, she was probably right. The females were smart enough to have long since flown south.

Deirdre was almost done with the perennials. She had just a bit more to do at the border. The daylilies were in desperate need of thinning as were those old standbys, wild geraniums. The geraniums came in a rainbow of colors. What a marvelous plant. Noticing that a small but growing number of invasive plants still remained, she decided to try to eliminate them before the blue jay determined she was worthy of attack. It was a race against time, and she knew it. Her father had been diligent about keeping the invasive plants under control. Given that the yard service did not attend to the flower beds, the invasive plants that had escaped weeding had long since scattered their seeds and proliferated. They were quickly taking over. It was definitely time to attend to them, lest the job become insurmountable. She thought, in passing, of her mother's friends, who definitely fit into the category of invasive plants. At least Ginny Finch did. Deirdre liked Stephanie

Lewis. She thought Stephanie was a good influence on her mother. But there definitely are people who occupy the invasive plant niche – once you have them, they are yours for life. Ginny Finch was like that. Deirdre was sure her mother had other friends like that too. But those were her mother's friends, weren't they? Who was she to judge?

Unable to resist, Deirdre turned to her favorite bed, the last one, the one that held the roses. Roses were in a category all by themselves. They were prima donnas. Roses could provide one with unmatched color and beauty – but only when one devotes endless hours and meticulous attention to them. They were worth it. The rose beds were her father's true love. He had had roses of every color and variety. Deirdre was particularly fond of the gallicas. She wondered if she had remembered to put them on the order list. She would have to mention that to Jeremy the next time she spoke to him. Anything that smelled that divine was nothing to dismiss. Her father had attended to his roses faithfully, feeding them once a month from April to August and mounding them with salt hay at the end of the season to protect them from the bitter cold of winter. It was quite clear her mother had not done any such thing. It was fortunate that there had been heavy snowfall the past two years. Ironically, snow protects plants from the winter cold, almost like a somewhat wet, white blanket.

All Deirdre could do at this point was clean the beds and hope that they would look respectable and well tended when the house went on the market. She could at least mound them for winter protection. Deirdre resolved that she would go to the garden store and buy salt hay or even cornhusks to protect the roses. Even though it was New

England, one could never count on blizzards or even light snow. She felt relaxed. She knew there was a lot more to be done, but she had started the work in the most appropriate way she knew. She would do a little more work before she went inside.

Deirdre thought that, if she could finish with the beds immediately surrounding the house, she would have accomplished the majority of the yard work.

At that point, Caroline emerged from the house and expressed her surprise at the condition of the yard. "You've done yeoman's work out here. Are you hungry?"

For Deirdre, getting things done had priority over eating. She was honest in her response. "No. I fortified myself with lots of fruit and honey. I'm almost done with the garden. I'll grab a bite when I come in. Are you in the mood for the supermarket? I only need a little rest. Then I'll be ready to shop."

"I'll talk to Penelope. We just had a late breakfast, so we can go after you rest up and have a little more to eat. Do you want me to have anything ready for when you come in?" Having slept in, Caroline was anxious to assuage her guilt and be helpful.

Deirdre was happy not to have to make her own lunch. "Just make me a sandwich. That will be totally adequate. See you in ten." With that, she hurried on to the final bed, ready to give it perfunctory attention. After that last bed was finished, she went over the garden in her mind. She had covered many different plants, an assortment of types and temperaments of people, and had relived many fond moments. She realized that she had gained from her father not only a profession but a philosophy as well.

THE SUPERMARKET

Deirdre had made serious inroads in the garden. Caroline and Penelope were well rested. Armed with the list so carefully drawn up the previous day, the group headed for the supermarket to buy the food they would need while they were staying at the house on Round Hill Road. Everyone was quite aware that it is a bad idea go food shopping on an empty stomach. Caroline and Penelope had eaten a late and substantial breakfast not that long before. Deirdre put two sandwiches under her belt after her marathon gardening efforts. They were prepared to buy a hefty amount of food and to have a hefty bill to go with it. Deirdre would be in the house for a number of weeks. She expected that this trip would cover the first few. She was convinced that she would use up the majority of the staples they bought and the ones already in the cupboards. From experience, Deirdre knew she would do more snacking once she was alone in the house. Anything that she didn't use would go to Emily.

Thinking about her waistline, she hoped that she would be leaving quite a bit for Emily and her family.

When Deirdre, Caroline, and Penelope arrived at the store, Deirdre was dismayed to find it wasn't the same old supermarket. There was no reason to expect that it would be. Caroline and Penelope had seen it since it's transformation into a much more upscale establishment, but the difference was disconcerting to Deirdre, mainly for sentimental reasons. Deirdre had loved going there with her father. As a teenager, one of her jobs had been to make sure that the kitchen was always well stocked. At the beginning, she and her father had gone to the supermarket together. After she'd gotten used to the task, he had driven her there and left her to do the shopping by herself. The job became routine. Once she got her driver's license, she was able to go alone and no longer needed her father as chauffeur.

The town's population growth and demographic shift meant that there would be a much wider, oftentimes ethnic selection of foods. That was good, given that all three of them had different eating habits. The new demographic of the town also meant that hardly anybody was in the store that Deirdre would be likely to know. Given the length of time since she had lived there, that was going to be true anyway. Most midday shoppers were seniors. She shopped with the hope of running into the mother of a former classmate – any former classmate. She'd had so many dinners at friends' houses during her high school years that she was more than familiar with most of her friends' mothers. She could even remember a lot of their dinner specialties.

The last person Deirdre expected to bump into was Mr. Remington. He was, instead, the first person they encountered. Assuming Deirdre might have a long conversation with him, Penelope and Caroline headed off to continue the shopping in another aisle. They were also quite happy to avoid talking to him themselves.

Mr. Remington had been the principal during Deirdre's latter years of high school and throughout the younger ones' entire school years. He had also been her English teacher her sophomore year. She felt a little thrill of expectation go through her when she saw him. She remembered, at graduation, when she'd received her diploma from him, she had been grateful she would never have to see him again. Now she was excited to see him. It was irony at its best, or at least its simplest. She would have expected to see a gray-haired version of the forty-five-year-old man she had known and was surprised to see a different person. True to expectation, he now had gray hair. There just was less of it. But his now deeply lined face had bushy eyebrows – a feature he'd not had during high school. Where did they come from? Were they a product of age? Could she one day wake up to see Jeremy had bushy eyebrows and realize they were old? What an exciting prospect.

She approached Mr. Remington with trepidation and greeted him, not as the youthful person that he had known, but the full-fledged adult she now was. They both were surprised – he at the fact that she was a mature adult, she at the fact that he seemed pleased to see her. He raised his bushy eyebrows. "Miss Lincoln, I haven't seen you in a long time. You must be living out of state."

"I am, Mr. Remington. I own a small nursery near Seattle."

"How charming. I once visited that part of the country. And a nursery? I never thought it stopped raining long enough to garden."

After that, they only chatted briefly. Deirdre wasn't sure she wanted the conversation to continue anyway. In any case, she was dumfounded there was, really, so little to say. She all of a sudden realized she was probably a vague memory at best. With that knowledge, she quickly wrapped up the encounter and hurried to catch up with Caroline and Penelope. She had just had another lesson – that she was not as memorable as she might have thought and, maybe, hoped.

After Deirdre's encounter with her old nemesis, the poetry they had studied that year and the passages from Shakespeare she had had to commit to memory came inexplicably flooding back. Remembering how he had told the class that they would appreciate knowing these things in later life, she wanted to run back and deliver Hamlet's soliloquy to him.

Deirdre spied her sisters in the condiment aisle. She hustled to join them. Even in two months, she could not imagine using up an entire bottle of mustard or of ketchup. Neither could she imagine doing without them. Those were the only condiments she could think they would need.

During her brief encounter with Mr. Remington, Caroline and Penelope had polished off most of the shopping. This "new" supermarket had all the ethnic foods that all three of them could want, as well as enough prepared meals to feed them well while still allowing them the time needed to work in the house. The remaining items on the list could be found in the substantial bulk section, the presence of which was new to Deirdre. Bulk food was commonplace in the Northwest, but she hadn't expected to find it in the store they had always frequented in North Linton.

With plummeting realization, Deirdre tallied up their purchases and came to a rough estimate. This really was going to be a costly shopping trip. They had spent a small fortune, but they agreed it was worth it. They had not yet bought any produce. After the supermarket, they planned to go to a store that, in their youth, had only been a vegetable stand. There, they would supplement the vegetables Uncle David had given them with enough for the rest of the week. They bought fruit at the supermarket because, although they were going to a local produce store, aside from apples, there was no good fruit to be found in New England in October. There wouldn't be a wide selection at the vegetable and fruit stand either.

After checking out, off to the vegetable store they went. That ramshackle, disorganized enterprise had undergone a radical transformation since any of the three had shopped there. The old owner of the vegetable stand, Mr. Pellegrino, had turned that familiar old business over to his daughter, Antonia. He'd had little choice if he wanted to keep the business in the family. His sons, Tommy and Gianni, had a prosperous law practice in Boston, leaving little time for anything else. The merchandizing of produce didn't fit in with their mind-sets. The sons were still of the generation that expected wives to serve up carefully prepared meals.

They certainly did not think about fruit or vegetables. They only thought about food in terms of what was on the dinner table. Little did the old-world gentleman, with his old-world attitude toward women, ever expect to turn over his precious business to a female.

Antonia had expanded the business and made it much more successful than her father ever had. It was now a solid business in a sturdy building. Antonia had supervised the construction of the building, seeing to it that it was tailored to the vegetable and fruit business. The new store was a joy to shop in. Deirdre thought, with regret, of the difficulties she'd had as a teenager shopping for produce, especially in the winter. This place would be a delight.

With the successes from both the supermarket and the glorious new produce stand behind them, the sisters went back to the old house. They had been right; it had been an expensive expedition, but it had also been interesting and worthwhile. Now, they were faced with putting the load of groceries away. An intriguing start to their week together.

THE MASTER BEDROOM

THE DOOR OF THE MASTER BEDROOM HAD BEEN KEPT closed the entire time since their mother had died. None of Claire's daughters needed any further reminders of what had happened. Deirdre thought that she should start working in that room before Caroline and Penelope returned to their respective homes. Even though Emily would still be close at hand after the others left, there were things that all four of them needed to make decisions about together, things that meant a great deal to them all but wouldn't necessarily mean much to anyone else.

As Deirdre headed upstairs, she sensed she had a shadow behind her. Solomon had not been in the master bedroom for a week and was extremely put out about it. As Deirdre opened the door, Solomon dashed into the bedroom ahead of her. Sunlight poured through the south window, leaving a rectangle of warmth on the floor. He obviously knew it would be there and had missed it. He lay down to soak up the rays, stretching out and rolling over, happily absorbing the heat of the sun. "Oh, sweetie. You have been deprived of your morning warmth. How have you kept up your spirits?" She suspected that the different, and probably improved, diet had something to do with his good mood. He certainly seemed to be purring a lot, more than he probably previously had.

The room's closed door and southern exposure combined to make it toasty. She had to deliberate whether or not to close the door to keep the room warm or to leave the door open in the hope that one or both of her sisters would join her at some point. She opted for warmth. Although Solomon could not talk, he would certainly have agreed with her.

There was general agreement that Deirdre had the least emotional stake in cleaning out the master bedroom. She did feel a little uncomfortable with that knowledge, but nothing was going to change that fact now. When she began to work in the room, however, she was surprised at the emotions that enveloped her. Those emotions, though, had so much more to do with her father than her mother. She was surprised at that. When would she ever stop mourning her father? She knew that she would always miss him, but surely the pangs would, at some point, subside.

Deirdre thought it would be most practical to start out by tackling her mother's jewelry box. She made small piles for each of her sisters, according to their mother's will. The rings went into the separate piles, one ring for each of them. The four of them had previously discussed the rest of the jewelry and had come to some preliminary decisions about how to apportion it. Deirdre could envision her mother in so many of the pieces. Memories of the necklace with the butterfly inside held a special place in her imagination. She couldn't remember a time when that necklace had not captivated her. She was delighted that her mother, remembering how much she loved it, had left it to her. That thoughtfulness was extraordinary … and totally out of character.

Deirdre was also pleased that the dress watch went to Caroline. She had always loved and coveted the watch with the opal face but wasn't ever serious about owning it. Deirdre never wore a watch. She could tell the time of day with an accuracy of twenty minutes without ever looking at a watch – another result of being a gardener and having a close relationship with the sun. The opal watch would never have seen the light of day had she owned it. And Penelope would get the pearls. With them, she would look particularly stunning as she made exquisite music. Uncle David was right with his suggestion about them.

Caroline and Emily would get most of the rest of the jewelry. It was almost as though their mother had known that neither Deirdre nor Penelope would be comfortable wearing expensive jewelry. Only Emily had that kind of social life. Having better jewelry meant that Caroline could look better as she attended high-end fundraisers in Washington. After finishing the more obvious distribution, Deirdre was still faced with a number of pieces to be allocated. Those went into a pile that the four of them would have to negotiate over.

The top of the bureau held more treasures to be divided. The dressing table silver caught Deirdre's eye. It actually came from their maternal grandmother and would be hotly contested for obvious, or not so obvious, reasons. She and Emily had preened in front of the mirror for hours when they were little. By the time Caroline came along, their mother, realizing the precious heirlooms were not toys, had put them out of sight. This would mainly be an issue between her older sister and herself.

Next, she opened the closet door and immediately had to take a step back. She had known vaguely what she was getting, but the sheer number of dresses, skirts, blouses, and shirts in the closet overwhelmed her. She and Jeremy would have to step up their social life if she ever wanted to do this wardrobe justice. She would now be prepared for anything. It hit her that she had a lot of folding up to do. Initially, it made sense for her to mail a lot of packages of clothes home. Jeremy would hate hanging it all up once it got there, but when he realized how much they'd never have to buy, he might be less irritated. Now, knowing the number of clothes she was dealing with, she made the decision that her new wardrobe would travel across the country with Jeremy and herself. She would only fold a few that she would wear on the cross-country trip.

Slowly, she folded those few. She pictured her parents at cocktail parties, dinners, the theatre and any number of other events. What an exciting life they must have had. There were enough shawls, scarves and hats – those things that fit any size – that her sisters would have a lot to choose from. She put those items in a separate pile for her sisters. There was no need to be greedy. The only thing her mother did not have a lot of was work clothes. No pants, no flannels. Not a surprise. God forbid that her mother should sweat.

Deirdre would still need to buy a few warm incidentals soon. She had brought all of her warm clothes, now supplemented by her mother's wardrobe, but her mother's clothes, although elegant for the most part, just weren't warm enough for cold New England weather, certainly not for the cold nights. She wondered how her mother had survived those nights. She knew that it was not from being warm-blooded. Deirdre needed something snuggly. She had known there were gaps that needed to be plugged. Now it was time to plug them.

It was clear that emptying the closet of clothes was more her problem alone. The rest of the room concerned them all. With that understanding, Deirdre turned her attention to the bedside table. There, she found her mother's most recent diary. Her mother had kept a diary, a five-year one, for as long as she could remember. Now she was intrigued, but she hesitated, having never seen any of the entries and feeling as if she would, even now, be invading privacy.

Slowly, she started to read. The entry she read must have taken place in a bad week. It was particularly uneventful. Deirdre read on about chance meetings at the grocery store and other downtown places. There were even entries about dinner menus. She looked back at the previous year, skimming through the pages for something substantive, but nothing popped out. Where was the emotion? There didn't seem to be any personal flavor. No texture. Her curiosity was aroused. She turned a few more pages. Still the same drivel.

Then she happened on the date her father had died. "Derek died today. Heart attack. I don't know what I am going to do without him. Forty-four mostly good years."

That was all? Deirdre was disappointed, to say the least. She would have thought there would be more after forty-four years. Granted, an earth-shattering event had just occurred, but if her mother was dispassionate enough to write at all, she could have put a little more into it. Deirdre had all her emotions wrapped up in what she was reading. She was not ready for more and, actually, was ready to stop working in that room for the day, though some work still remained. Her spirits sank as she had her long-held suspicions about her mother confirmed. There had not been great depth to Claire's personality. Surely, that had not always been the case. Tossing all this around in her head, she headed for the door.

All of a sudden, the pictures on the wall struck her. She had not thought about them before. They were like rugs. Or paint. They blended in, a part of the house's structure, or so it seemed. For the first time, she truly grasped that her job was to remove the stamp of the past forty years. But that was for another day. She had accomplished a lot and strained her emotions to the limit. She felt overloaded. Even though working on the closet was wrought with memories, she would continue at a future time, with the knowledge that the majority of the closet's contents were now hers.

She was surprised to find that it was still early. The day was yet young. Perhaps she and Penelope could go downtown, shop for the warm clothes she still needed, and take care of various other small items. Deirdre wanted to spend as much time as possible with Penelope. Her younger sister was such delightful company but would soon be returning to Hartford. Deirdre left the master bedroom, feeling satisfied with what she had accomplished. She was also comfortable that what remained could be done after everyone had left. Besides, the sun had moved around so it no longer made it a warm spot for Solomon. They would both be back another day.

Shopping Downtown

THE CENTRAL DOWNTOWN WAS NOW A MYSTERY TO Deirdre. She wanted to take this opportunity to see what the old familiar streets held, to mosey around and find out which shops remained from the old days. She knew that the old department store was still there. That was where her mother had died. Penelope had seen the changes the center had undergone, at least most of them, but this would be Deirdre's first trip downtown since she had arrived. She needed the break from working in the house. This need did not bode well for her efforts to prepare the house for sale.

Deirdre and Penelope set out to accomplish their various goals, most of them Deirdre's. Deirdre backed the car out of the driveway. It was not the easiest one to navigate, but she needed to get good at doing it once again. One side of the driveway was lined with a thick hedge, lush and green. The lawn sloped up toward the house on the other side. They reached the bottom with only two near misses. After that, it was straight sailing. It was a fairly short drive to downtown, although the streets were filled with more traffic than either one of them expected or, certainly, was used to. Once they reached the heart of downtown, they looked for a parking space. Finding a place to park was not as easy as it once had been. While they both had initially thought the new demographic was a positive development, what with the greater choice in the supermarket, now Deirdre cursed the population growth.

Quickly scanning the main street for recognizable shops, Deirdre saw the store where they had all bought their Girl Scout paraphernalia. Unconsciously, she heaved a sigh of relief at the sight. It was a mystery to her why she had done this, but she had saved her Girl Scout sash and still knew exactly where it was. The sash held her many and varied badges, remnants from that store in that part of her life. Like most girls in her troop, she had not used the scouting experience to explore new areas. Instead, in the pursuit of badges, she had only chosen to broaden her knowledge in areas where she already had some comfort. She had completed the cooking badge with very little effort, knocked off others that would be considered in the domestic category, gathered a few hobby-related ones and excelled at outdoors skills – gardening, wildlife, even the simpler outdoor sports. Deirdre asked Penelope if she still had her Girl Scout sash. Penelope answered, regretfully, "It's been years since I saw it. I have to admit I've always suspected Mother threw it out. A lot of my stuff went inexplicably missing over the years."

That brought the subject of the Girl Scout store,

as they'd always called it, to a close. Deirdre had never bought anything else there, although the clothes had been quite respectable. At the time when she was that age, she had been getting hand-me-downs from two of her three sisters. Penelope said she had suffered from the same problem. It had been a red-letter day when either one of them got clothes that were brand new. Deirdre wondered why she had never gotten cast-offs from her mother as well. Then she realized those clothes were too worldly. Where did they go then?

They went into Webber's department store to get the warm clothes – nightgown and knee socks – that Deirdre wanted and needed. These items were not often needed in the Northwest, a fact Deirdre kept reminding herself whenever she wondered why she lived so far from New England. She would enjoy this year, but perhaps *enjoy* was the wrong word. Considering the harsh climate, *savor* that she did not have to live there permanently was more like it. They spent a lot of time looking at knee socks and decided on more than were needed for the present. The selection was too tempting. What she wanted was just not available in the Northwest.

Next, they turned their attention to nightgowns. What a varied collection – every color and style. There were so many. There were even sexy ones. After spending a lot of time choosing the perfect one, Deirdre turned to purchase it. In a serendipitous moment, Deirdre bumped into a woman laden with shopping bags. This woman had obviously been shopping all day long. And it was only early afternoon. The downtown had more and more interesting wares than ever before. New businesses had moved in when old establishments had closed. There were stores tucked away in unexpected places. No wonder this shopper had so many bags.

Stopping to apologize, Deirdre was struck by the notion that the woman was more than a little familiar. This woman was plump in a svelte sort of way and very attractive. After not much searching through her memory bank, Deirdre realized she was looking at Veronica Dylan, the mother of one of her close grammar school friends. A whole host of memories came along with the recognition. This was the woman who had made the spaghetti sauce that stood out in her childhood. Maybe Deirdre should tell her. Deirdre was sure she had never complimented her on it before, so it would be a pleasant surprise to Mrs. Dylan. Deirdre could even get the recipe. A win-win situation anyway one looked at it.

Mrs. Dylan was also a nurse. She had attended to Grandfather Lincoln in his final illness. There was clearly a lot to talk about with this chance encounter. For starters, she dearly wanted to know how her friend, Marilyn, was, and what she was up to. She knew that Marilyn had two children but had lost track of their ages. She was astounded to learn that the oldest was now in high school. Where had the time gone? Mrs. Dylan beamed with pride as she told Deirdre that her younger granddaughter had just been inducted into the National Honor Society. This was an example, unlike most, of justifiable grandparent pride. Deirdre was not surprised at the information; Marilyn had been no slouch at her studies. She had obviously passed her brains down to the next generation.

Deirdre tore herself away from what was, to her, an

encounter that was an unexpected delight. As Deirdre and Penelope took the elevator down to the ground floor, Penelope's attention was caught by the fact that they were passing the music department. Just in the nick of time, they decided to stop.

Molly needed to supplement the little sheet music available at the house. The music department would have sheet music Molly could use. With the music they bought for her, she could learn to play more sophisticated pieces. The range of possibilities for Molly was limitless. Both Deirdre and Penelope wanted to foster this new avenue for their niece. Deirdre had always regretted that she had not been more diligent when her parents had given her the opportunity to play the piano. She could have become a concert pianist!

Once the elevator doors opened, they found themselves in an entirely different world. It was like being in a living room. A number of wing chairs were scattered about, with tables and magazines one could read while listening to peaceful music. They spent more time than they'd intended. They had a hard time settling on the right piece for Molly to start with because the choice was so large. Penelope recommended various pieces. The final choice was a Beethoven sonata. The only thing they could do was introduce Molly to great piano music. The rest was up to her.

By now, it was definitely past time for lunch. Even before they'd left the house, Deirdre and Penelope were aware they would go to Morgan's for lunch. Morgan's was an old-style restaurant that served true New England fare, especially milkshakes – none of this thick, modern stuff.

That was a frappe. In Rhode Island, this unadulterated beverage was called a cabinet. Here, at least, a milk shake had only milk and syrup. Morgan's also had Welsh rarebit, the kind of meal old ladies who smell like lavender eat for lunch on a daylong shopping trip. They did not have time to make this a daylong expedition, but Deirdre's stomach told her that a stop at Morgan's was long overdue.

After satisfying themselves with a traditional lunch, they continued on. Deirdre, looking for the stamp and coin store, was disappointed, but not surprised to find no trace of it. Was her generation the last to spend time with such diversions? She was sad to think that philately was dead. She was too young to be an old fart, but that's what this trip was telling her. Another badge for that Girl Scout sash. A badge for being an old fart. She had little doubt that she would have to design both the badge and the requirements herself.

As she lamented the disappearance of the stamp store, Deirdre's eye settled on First City Bank on the corner. She knew that her old beau, Jack Noel, was the bank's loan officer. Penelope chose to wait outside in the sun. Deirdre prepared to go inside, hoping that Jack would be there. Unconsciously, she found herself looking at her reflection in the bank window, fixing the wisps of hair that had been blown by the gentle breeze. She had the passing thought, *I'm a happily married woman. Why am I so excited?* Then she charged in.

First City was an old-fashioned bank from the past, as solid-looking as she had grown up believing all banks were. The counters were granite, polished, and sparkling. All around was brass trim. Even the ashtrays, unheard of in this day and age, were brass. Of course, smoking was no longer allowed.

She was in luck. Jack was sitting at his desk without a customer, a rarity at the busy branch. She was still feeling those inexplicable twinges of the past romance. Jack was as debonair as he had been in their high school days. He was attired in a conservative suit but chose to express his personality with less than conservative accessories. The only way she could describe his shirt was to say it was the color of St. Charles Place. To her, it screamed, *Jack!* He was much younger-looking than he had any right to be. It didn't seem fair. He looked up and registered recognition and pleasure at seeing her.

"Deirdre, what a delight to see you. I assumed you would be back in town. I was so sorry to read about your mother." She knew that he was sincere about his condolences. She could only believe that he was also sincere about his delight in seeing her. They had remained friends after high school, but he had ended up marrying a friend of Deirdre's, a girl of Chinese ancestry. Deirdre had always known that his eye was easily drawn to Asian women. That had been the reason they had broken up. Deirdre had been devastated. Claire had been decidedly less than sympathetic, letting Deirdre believe that she did not deserve Jack anyway. It was no surprise that Deirdre felt lacking, even today.

Rising to the occasion, she put on her brightest smile and asked, "How are you? How are Fanny and the kids?"

"We're doing really well. When our youngest was still in the oven, we built a house. It's about half a mile from Pellegrino's. We have a wooded lot. The older two are getting old enough to play outside by themselves. It sure helps not to have to worry about traffic."

"Or overdevelopment." She quickly estimated where their house was. "You're near the bogs, aren't you?"

"Yeah, and it's a lot more peaceful than in town; that's for sure."

A customer was waiting for Jack's attention, so Deirdre said her good-byes. "Give my best to Fanny. We'll have to get together before I leave town."

Deirdre left the bank to rejoin her sister. Penelope was seated on a bench and was reluctant to leave the warmth of her spot in the sun. Deirdre said she would only be gone briefly, and with that, she was on her way again. One more stop. Even though she had eaten a good-sized lunch, her stomach propelled her to look for the store that had sold lots of English goodies. No, it was not an oxymoron. She had learned about the store from Miriam. They had spent almost a decade reveling in its various treats.

But no more. There was not a trace of it. Where would people get trifle and meat pies? She knew that mincemeat, while not common, was not hard to find with a thorough search. And the rest?

There was no point in lingering further. She would have to keep the memories of that wonderful shop in her mind. She had already learned to make so many of those dishes anyway. Still, it was sad that the store was gone. Others needed to learn about the wonders of British cuisine.

It was time to stop dallying. She had seen what she wanted to of the downtown, bought the warm clothes she intended, and had even seen an old flame. What more could she possibly expect? With that, she collected Penelope. It was time to find the car. One more errand remained to be done before they got home. The thrift store where she could buy the needed heavy sweater was on the way. It would be more than useful for work in the attic and basement, not to mention just facing the autumn chill, which threatened to arrive at any time.

DEREK'S LIBRARY

FRIDAY MORNING, AFTER SHE GOT THE KIDS OFF TO school, Emily joined her sisters at the family home. Before they got down to work, Deirdre laid out the day's tasks. Every day had begun that way because, as the foreman, she was anxious to move things along. "Today, I'd like us to start in the library. It occurs to me that, while the four of us are still together, we should deal with the books and records and then move on to the smaller furniture. We only have today left to do this in person. Then, I guess we'll spend lots of time on the phone. Too bad Mother didn't let us sort through the books after Daddy died. I'd venture a guess she hasn't been in the library much since."

After settling on the plan for the day, the others went to the nearby liquor store to get cardboard boxes. Emily had planned to go alone, but at the last minute, Caroline and Penelope decided to accompany her to help expedite things. Deirdre mused about how, in Massachusetts, a liquor store is called a package store, as if giving weight to the adage that good things come in small packages. She went to the library to prepare for the upcoming work. It eased everyone's mind that what they were about to tackle that day wouldn't require them to get dirty – dusty, but not dirty. Knowing the job would be light, Deirdre was dressed in casual slacks and a light sweater. Her choice of sweater color was unintentional but seasonal; it was the same red as the old maple tree outside.

She almost tiptoed into the library, even though no one else was in the house. The carpet hadn't yet been removed, so her footsteps made no noise as she entered the room, the room that had also been their father's study. They had learned, at an early age, to be quiet and not disruptive when he was in his study working. Derek often brought work home to do after dinner. One of his daughters would keep him company, quietly reading while he worked on town business. Deirdre looked at the red leather chair in the corner and quietly sighed. She remembered the countless hours she had spent there, curled up, reading everything from Ludwig Bemelman's innocent *Madeline* to Marcel Proust's *Swann's Way* with its memory-unlocking madeleines dipped in tea. The smell of the leather chair would never leave her. The sense of smell is as connected to the olfactory nerve as the sense of taste. Proust was right. Both unveil memories. The chair and reading were inextricably connected in her mind. She could picture her father as she, as a small child, sat in his lap. In the recesses of her mind, Deirdre could still feel the wool of the suit he didn't change out of until bedtime. She had learned to read in his lap. She didn't remember the process, just that one day those squiggles magically became words.

Deirdre did not realize how long she had been lost in reverie when she heard the back door open and her sisters enter the kitchen. She felt guilty at how little she had accomplished in their absence. The library had not really needed much in the way of preparation, though. It was all set for them to begin dividing the books. Out of long-ingrained habit, she did not call out to her sisters but, rather, went to the kitchen to greet them.

After making appreciative comments about the number of boxes they had brought back, Deirdre started making recommendations about the book division. "I think the encyclopedias and all the children's books should go to Emily. C'mon back to the library. We can decide everything in greater detail there."

They trooped to the library. On the way, Deirdre continued. "Penelope, will you take all of the music books? Does anyone else want any specific music book? Composer biography? Opera librettos? If so, take it up with Penelope."

Worried her desires would be overlooked, Caroline broke in. "I'd like all the books on politics, or as many as I can have."

Deirdre was not willing to give up without a fight. "I'd like to have the two books about FDR and the one about JFK. Caroline, can I have those few? I'd also like to take the gardening books, but I'm more than happy to let someone else have any they want. I dearly want reference books, though. I'm not prepared to be quite so flexible with them."

Emily had been quiet until then. She chimed in, surprising her sisters who weren't accustomed to hearing her speak up for herself. "I've been searching for the book about French Gothic cathedrals. It never ceased to grab my attention. I hope it still will – if we can find it."

Distributing the rest of the books, while time-consuming, went without a problem. In a corner, they found the long-forgotten and much loved *Little Women*. That book, with its four sisters, had an eerie echo of the Lincoln family. Deirdre suggested that Emily, as the oldest, deserved the book. As the second oldest daughter, Deirdre ought to have been more of a tomboy. Jo, her counterpart in that book, certainly was. Deirdre was, at least, strong-willed. And opinionated. It was agreed by all four that Emily should take the book. It was also agreed that Deirdre was opinionated.

Deirdre had a flashback when they ran across another old book in the corner, one with the picture of an elk on the cover. She had taken that book with her to first grade. While the rest of the class learned about Spot, Dick, and Jane, she cried for most of three days. They had been learning to read; she was halfway through that book. No wonder she was short on patience. She learned that trait early. But patience was not required now. She was enjoying her sisters' company. By extension, she was enjoying the job at hand. This was not hard work. Nothing could take away the pleasure she was feeling. Books were commonplace treasures for all four.

They moved on to the language books. With only a slight tussle, the French books were divided between Emily, Caroline, and Penelope. Deirdre got all the Spanish books. Because the West has such a large population of Hispanics, she became fluent in their language. In high school, Caroline staked out the German language for herself. Nobody else in the family spoke that language, so she got all the German books.

The last book to be decided upon was the most contentious. Deirdre summed up the disposition of the book. "I guess we all have a claim to the Longfellow anthology. The first poem each of us learned was by Longfellow, but a different one for each of us. We'll have a battle for that book. Caroline, I remember when you asked Daddy if we could have a children's hour. At that point, you personified Allegra with your laughing eyes. You were such a happy little girl. And from then on, Daddy came home early so we could have that special hour." Deirdre smiled in recollection, as if it were yesterday.

Emily brought up the issue of cookbooks. "I know they're all in the kitchen, but there are a few cookbooks I still have an emotional attachment to. We bought a lot when I started cooking meals. Some I'd really like. And there's the international cookbook. That goes way back. Caroline, that one has your name written all over it — in crayon. You must have been five when you did your handiwork."

After the books, they moved on to records. That was a harder task. All four had bought music to replace records they had grown up with but each still had gaps in her collection. They couldn't skip the process entirely. It was, however, dealt with more reasonably than they had anticipated. A simple coin toss resolved the disposition when there were any disputes.

When they were done with the music, Deirdre jumped in again to steer their efforts. "Let's go to the living room and talk about small furniture. There's a lot to discuss. I think Penelope gets most of it. Caroline, you've said you only want the dry bar. Do you really mean that?"

The living room was definitely the place to finish the topic, as most of the better furniture was there. However, some good, small pieces were sprinkled throughout the rest of the house. Although each had sentimental attachments to particular pieces, Penelope's older sisters agreed that the bulk of the furniture should go to her.

Penelope blushingly reacted to her sisters' generosity. "You guys are being so thoughtful. I'm going to have to buy a house. Then, I suppose I'm going to have the money to do exactly that."

Deirdre suddenly blurted out. "Oh my God, we've not even discussed the pictures. They're something I thought about for the first time yesterday. Why don't we do the same thing with the pictures that we did with the music? We can choose the ones we would really love to have. As long as no one else also wants what we choose, it's ours. If more than one wants the same picture, then we can toss a coin. What do you think?"

"Well, we can proceed along those lines." Emily sounded pleased. "I think we've accomplished an awful lot today. Let's help Caroline box up her stuff. She'll be the first of us to take anything. I can't believe that will happen in just two days. That's not a lot of time to box it all up, so let's make a start now."

Deirdre tried to be cheerful, but she was sad. "Caroline, it's only been a week. Already I've gotten used to you again. You probably don't believe me, but I'm going to miss you, kiddo."

There were lots of nods and damp eyes. It had been the kind of time together that they had all needed.

"Let's go over to my house when we're done. We can have a big dinner. Or we could go out to eat. Maybe that's a better idea. I don't know about you, but I bet no one wants to cook. I sure don't." Emily left it to her sisters to decide where to eat.

With the prospect of a good dinner ahead, especially one they didn't have to cook, the packing went quickly. There was controversy over what type of food they wanted, but they finally settled on Greek. The prospect of baklava made them hurry.

Farewell for Now

After dragging her heels in the morning for the better part of a week, Deirdre had finally adjusted to East Coast time. It was still a rude shock to have to get up at seven. Caroline was going home later that morning, and a number of loose ends needed to be tied up before the departure. Tom, who had taken it upon himself to have a trailer hitch mounted on Claire's car, was driving Caroline to DC, her newly acquired possessions in tow. After an overnight rest, he would drive back to North Linton. As it stood, the trailer that Tom had rented the previous evening had yet to be filled.

After eating a Spartan breakfast with Caroline and Penelope, Deirdre packed food for Caroline and Tom to eat on the road. Tom and Caroline had a long drive ahead of them. The three sisters who had been staying in the house on Round Hill Road then started to pack the trailer. Caroline was not taking much furniture. As she had made abundantly clear, there was little of the furniture from the

Lincoln house that would fit in with her modern decor. It was beyond Deirdre's imagination how Caroline, who had grown up in a household with lovely antiques, should now have a fancy for the opposite extreme – modern design! Caroline was taking primarily boxes – boxes of books, boxes of kitchen paraphernalia, and boxes of dining room incidentals. She was also taking the couch and the dry bar, both of which would fit in nicely with her other furniture. Since Caroline was taking little else, Tom had been able to get a smaller trailer for the things she was taking.

Deirdre, Caroline, and Penelope were loading the trailer when Tom and Emily arrived. The three were passing boxes quickly along from one to the next in an assembly line to facilitate the loading process. Tom stepped to the front of the line as soon as they arrived. All three knew he had a better sense than they did of how to pack the trailer with the least potential for damage. He knew that too.

As the trailer filled up, snatches of conversation between the sisters filled the air. They were aware that they would see each other again quite soon, but so much had transpired in the week they had been together that each felt she had to sum up her feelings. They were feelings, however, that had always existed.

Emily started the conversation off. "These eight days have gone by too quickly. I don't know what I'm going to do without my little sisters. This has been better than growing up, because we're all big kids now. I do feel that I missed a big part of the week by not being here at night. I think we should all descend on Deirdre next – all at once. Will you be ready for us next year?"

Deirdre responded enthusiastically, brimming with

delight. "I can handle that. Promise you'll all come?" She knew that they would not all make the journey, but her hopes were raised anyway.

Caroline lit up. "What a great idea."

"I'm ready." Penelope seemed excited about the plan.

After Tom had been packing the trailer for a short period, Deirdre and Caroline went inside the house for water. Finding herself temporarily alone with her younger sister, Deirdre took the opportunity to pick up a thread that had been lying around loose the entire week. "I sometimes feel that Em and I represent an entirely different litter from you and Penelope."

Caroline gave her a searching look. "What do you mean by that?"

"We come from a part of Mother's life whose characteristics are poles apart from the part of her life you're from. I don't think that your memories are the same as ours at all."

Caroline didn't understand what Deirdre was getting at. "But we all grew up together."

Deirdre tried to explain. "Each of us presented her with very different challenges. She had to react to widely varying circumstances over the years. Mother seemed never to change. She was the same person all along. We didn't question that at that time. Now it's a bit odd. How could that be? Isn't life usually an evolutionary process? Anyway, at least we know that now. That's a good jumping off point for all of us. Let's go on, having learned a vital, but tardy, piece of information."

They all liked each other, something not always found in families. The entire week had been the culmination of more than a quarter century of collective experience. A new leaf had truly been turned. Deirdre hoped most of their feelings were now out in the open. She had done her best to see that was true.

Caroline and Deirdre returned to find the trailer was close to full and not much left to be packed. Tom had a good eye for fitting things in without wasting space. With all the hands, no one had broken much of a sweat. At least Tom and Caroline would have Jonathan's help to unload when they arrived. Not quite as many hands but adequate help nonetheless. It would be too late to return the trailer until the next morning. Tom would do that before starting off on his return trip.

Once the trailer was full and after an adequate rest, Tom and Caroline got in the car and pulled out of the driveway with the trailer in tow. Formal good-byes were not necessary. They would see each other in a short time. Everyone waved – Emily, Deirdre, and Penelope standing in the driveway watching the car recede, Caroline looking backward until she could no longer see her sisters.

❧

Penelope would be the next to leave. On Monday, she had an important rehearsal, one she could not miss. In not too much time, the orchestra would unveil the Mendelssohn concerto. She knew her part but had only played it a few times with the full orchestra. New pieces always took time to smooth out.

Penelope was planning to take some boxes now and the remainder at a later date. To get Penelope off to an early start the following day, Emily was staying to help pack Penelope's goods. Penelope would need to hire a moving company to get the rest to Connecticut. Emily left to go get Molly, who had been at home with the twins while their parents were helping Caroline's departure. The twins would be spending the afternoon with friends, enabling Molly to join her mother and aunts.

Now it was Penelope's turn to pack up her books, linens, and other small items. But along with those things, Penelope and Molly were going to sort through the sheet music and decide who would get what. Penelope had a small upright piano in her apartment. Now that Molly also had a piano, the sheet music had to be divided. Although Penelope was not proficient at piano, she knew what she wanted to learn to play. Some pieces *demanded* they be played on that instrument.

Penelope's car was soon packed. Although she was getting more from the house than any of her sisters, the bulk of her new possessions would temporarily remain in North Linton. After a day that wasn't terribly strenuous, they decided to retire to Emily's house and relax. The twins had been on their own for a long time. Emily was suffering a mother's guilt. Besides, Penelope wanted one more evening with her nieces and nephew. She had also been away from home long enough and was definitely ready to resume her normal routine. They were more tired than they would have expected. Emily decided to make her farewell that evening.

Deirdre and Penelope returned to Round Hill Road. They both turned in early. When they woke up in the morning, Penelope did not waste a lot of time preparing for her departure. After a shorter time than expected, she was ready to hit the road. The car was already set to go. When Deirdre said good-bye, she hoped that she was saying good-bye to Penelope's car for the last time. She suspected she might be.

Deirdre was now, more or less, on her own. She would have Emily's help, but the majority of the work would now be up to her.

THREE

Working Alone

For two weeks after Caroline and Penelope went home, Deirdre enjoyed unseasonably warm weather. Although she relished the gentler days, experience told her the weather would not cooperate much longer. She was right. Over the preceding week, the days had been getting chillier. Just the day before, there had been a cold snap.

Fall was rapidly descending. The transition was unmistakable. Deirdre had not experienced that seasonal transition for many years. The trees had shed their finery, as if they had just come home from a ball. They had disrobed with wanton disregard, strewing their leaves everywhere. The sides of the roads and most lawns were inundated with the leaves that so recently lit up the landscape with a riot of bright colors. Raking was a never-ending task for homeowners, most of whom ignored the job altogether. They knew the effort would only be futile. It had always been that way. As little girls, Deirdre and Caroline had made big piles of leaves and jumped into them with great delight. Deirdre was sure Emily had done the same thing. It's a rite all young children, both girls and boys, enjoy in the fall.

To Deirdre, the nakedness of the trees indicated that the peak of the fall was already past. Right on target, she had the sinking feeling that went along with the shorter days. At least these days in North Linton would not be as short as they would be at home. When she returned to the Northwest, she would not be forced to face the bitter cold. She would, however, have to put up with the dreary darkness that began early in the afternoon. Where she and Jeremy lived, the winters days were as short as those in northern Europe.

Deirdre had been on the East Coast for over a month. She once again thought of it as being home. *Home.* There was that word again. Deirdre had spent her days in North Linton reliving a time in a home from the past. She would soon be returning to the present, to her current home. The time was passing quickly, more so than she realized. Her days had been consumed with going through the contents of the house and organizing those contents for dispersal.

She had not yet been in the attic on this trip, but it was on that day's agenda. She knew she could not put the job off indefinitely, and if she waited much longer, the attic would be too cold.

The attic could be sweltering in the summer. It could require a double layer of clothes after November. Now, all that was necessary was a heavy sweater. But it was questionable how much longer that would be true. Deirdre was relieved that she had bought a warm sweater at the secondhand store. The attic itself was distinctly separate from the rest of the house. Its entrance was an unusual one. A long chain with a metal ring at its end hung from the ceiling in the hallway on the second floor. Pulling the chain opened a ceiling panel that revealed a sliding staircase. It was that staircase that led to the attic. Deirdre pulled the chain, slid the staircase down, and prepared herself mentally for what she was about to encounter.

As she ascended the stairs, the smell of the attic met her. It was the same smell she'd encountered the first time she had ever been up there – clean but dry and woody. *How could that be?* she asked herself. She would have thought that forty years' worth of household smells would have permeated the attic. But then, it was separate from the rest of the house. Still, the aroma said *home*.

The attic was a sea of cardboard boxes, punctuated now and then by old, well-remembered pieces of furniture. So much more was there since her father had died. In rearranging so many of the upstairs rooms, her mother must have put a lot of those rooms' old contents in containers and had them moved to the attic – out of sight, out of mind. Deirdre wondered if her mother had done the remodeling just to erase reminders of the past or if she had been simply following her own whims. Deirdre suspected it was the latter. Now Deirdre was facing the same sort of job that should have been done two years before.

None of the boxes was labeled, but Deirdre was sure that the attic was full of relics from her and her sisters' respective childhoods and adolescences. She could only imagine that each box contained items related to the furniture it surrounded. Ignoring the need to look at anything that was likely from Penelope's and Caroline's rooms, Deirdre was drawn to the boxes next to a bookcase that had been in her own bedroom. When she opened the first carton, she found her suspicions confirmed. It did, in fact, contain books. Most of the books in that first box were collections of short stories. She pulled out a couple that made her flush with pleasure. There was her treasured copy of *Aesop's Fables*. What a lovely book – not big but imaginatively illustrated and, no great surprise, full of simple truths. Among the many books of short stories was another of her favorites, Rudyard Kipling's *Just So Stories*.

The best book, though, was a simple one with stories appealing to the childish imagination. She had read stories from that book long after one would expect. She read them to her younger sisters, not because she was a good older sister but because she loved the stories. One from the children's stories was about a baker whose bread got so big it escaped from the oven. The bread ultimately rose to the sky. That is apparently where cumulus clouds came from. The explanation seemed to make as much sense as anything else. Another story that stood out in her mind was called "Cheese, Peas, and Chocolate Pudding." The little boy in that story wouldn't eat anything but cheese, peas, and chocolate pudding. For three days, he was Deirdre's hero, rescuing her from, among other things, the dreaded broccoli. Then, the fourth day came, and her parents decided it was time to stop humoring her.

Deirdre shuffled through the rest of the books, looking for another that had given her solace as well as pleasure when she had been young. In that one, three children, whose mother had died, spend their spare time playing in their father's hardware store. They devise imaginary scenarios and dress in costumes made up from the contents of the store – a saucepan for a helmet, a dishtowel for a shirt, a cookie sheet for a shield. Then the children's father remarries. Life becomes difficult for them. Deirdre couldn't remember a lot of the story, but she did remember that their new stepmother was unkind, almost to the point of being cruel. The happy ending had the children turning into swans and paddling away into the sunset. She felt a special connection to the story because the eldest sister was named Deirdre. At those times when she felt particularly alienated from her mother, the ending resonated. It seemed, at those times, that there really was a way out. She had always felt that she had a magical escape. She had forgotten about that book when she first moved out, hadn't felt that it was appropriate to search for it immediately after her father's death, and now realized this would be her last chance to find it. She knew she should not get her hopes up. But they'd elevated anyway.

Deirdre hadn't had a lot of toys in those days, just a lot of great books. As Claire became less anxious to spend time with daughters who were becoming more independent and less compliant, she became increasingly remote. As that happened, Deirdre's younger sisters had received an increasing number of toys. Deirdre had wanted more toys but hadn't gotten them. She had been at that in-between age when toys would not be wanted much longer anyway. She now realized that she had been the luckier one. Now there was a treasure trove of books.

She opened another nearby box and was rewarded

with memories from the seventh grade. In that school year, she had won a spelling bee and placed in the science fair. She found the booklet of challenging words to spell, the chart she drew of the various acid and alkaline substances she tested as part of her science fair project, and even the litmus paper! She found too the much loved Halloween drawing from the art teacher she'd had and adored that year. She had not understood Miss Cameron's lack of interest in dating her other favorite teacher, Mr. Egan. Nor had she even heard the word lesbian at that time. It was only recently that she had learned that he too was gay. Oh the wonders of innocence.

Nestled underneath all the other things in the last box from her room were two of her favorite stuffed animals. She was reminded of a play that she was in when she was in the third grade. Rabbit was the main ingredient in the stone soup that the peasant woman made using the recipe of the vagabond who had stopped for food at her farmhouse kitchen. Deirdre had taken her stuffed rabbit to school with her to be used as a prop in the play. She was as relieved to find it now as she had been then to safely bring it home when the play was over.

Deirdre was surprised that, for now, there wasn't much more to do in the attic. Only a handful of boxes were left to be opened. She and her sisters had taken as much of their belongings as they could when each had first moved out. They still had to contend with all the furniture that had made its way up from the second-floor rooms, but there weren't many boxes left to explore. Knowing she would be back on a future day, she left the attic and folded up the stairs.

Feeling guilty, Deirdre knew she owed Solomon some attention. After every meal, she had tried to spend some time with him, but he was standoffish. His attention requirements were limited to being fed and being in the same room as her. Spending time in the master bedroom together served them both well. Solomon would get that needed attention, and Deirdre would be able to continue her work there. With any luck, she'd be able to wrap up her efforts in that room by the end of the day. So that's where she headed next.

Solomon's keen ears picked up the noise of Deirdre's footsteps as she walked along the second-floor hallway, approaching the door of the master bedroom. He slowly strolled up to her and rubbed against her leg. Cats will avoid appearing needy at all costs, even if they are. When she opened the door, he headed toward the upholstered chair and jumped up, snuggling into a comfortable position.

While Solomon was settling in, Deirdre cast an appraising glance around the room. Her eyes lit, first, on the round bedside table. On its lower shelf lay a small stack of books, the only books in the room. She had missed them before. Curious, she shuffled through them. Three were in the coffee table book category. Two of those were memorabilia of trips Claire and Derek had taken together, trophy books really. Claire had clearly bought the third shortly before she died, in anticipation of her planned trip with Stephanie Lewis and Ginny Finch. The book was a compilation of photographs of covered bridges, whitewashed churches, and historic houses throughout Vermont. That one would be right up Penelope's alley, Vermont being a straight shot north for her.

Just a few noteworthy items remained, not really many, considering the length of time Claire had lived in the house. The very first Mother's Day present Caroline had given Claire, without doubt purchased by Derek, was a medium-sized ceramic piggy bank. It sat proudly atop Claire's bureau, and it would probably mean a great deal to Caroline to get it back.

Most interesting were four small containers the size of cigar boxes Claire kept in the bottom drawer of her dresser. Each contained a kindergarten picture, identifying whose box it was. Random childhood mementos were thrown into each box. What struck Deirdre was that hers was nearly empty, save for a small necklace of pink beads with white beads that had letters spelling Lincoln in the middle and a teething ring with her name inscribed on an attached silver hanging tag. The former was to make sure she didn't go home with the wrong parents; the latter was to ensure she didn't unduly annoy the parents she did go home with. Surely, there were other parts of her childhood that were more memorable than that. Deirdre put the boxes aside, where she could easily give them to their new owners. Then, she scooped up Solomon and, pleased with what she had accomplished, shut the door and went downstairs.

HOUSE FOR SALE

The local Realtors seemed to have an innate sense of propriety. The Lincolns were an old, well known, and respected family in town. The majority of the real estate establishment had, at one time or another, had dealings with the town manager's office and, therefore, with Derek. Many of the younger real estate agents had been classmates of Deirdre or one of her sisters. So the family was left alone to do its grieving. But the house had many qualities that made it a *hot* property. It was sizeable, well maintained, and located in a quiet residential neighborhood, all of which meant the house would get a lot of attention. They would not be left alone for long.

Emily didn't start getting calls until three weeks after the funeral. But when the phone started ringing, the calls came fast and furious. After the third call, Emily phoned Deirdre. Her message was simple. "The vultures have started circling."

The family had a large choice of Realtors to work

with, the whole array of local professionals. Uncle David had done good spadework though. He researched the possibilities and chose a Realtor who was well known for both her integrity and her success. She was ready on the day they selected.

Before the Realtor showed up, Emily arrived at the house on Round Hill Road midmorning, leaving enough time to discuss the entire process with Deirdre. Both their hearts were a little bit heavy. They settled on an asking price, what they should leave in the house to show it well, the timing they hoped for, and all the other necessary details that had to be decided upon.

Before they could even start to talk about the sale of the family house, Deirdre had news of her own. "It turns out there are a lot of real estate transactions going on. Jeremy called last night. We've been hoping to expand the nursery for the past year. We now have an opportunity we can't pass up. Our next-door neighbors are getting on in years. They've decided to move to a retirement community. They knew that we wanted to grow and have asked us if we want to buy their place. We'd hoped for this property but thought we'd have to wait another few years. It's a great deal for both of us. Without even going through a Realtor, we have the chance to buy. That saves them the commission fees and lets them sell it to us at a much lower price."

"Sounds wonderful. What else?" Emily's curiosity was piqued.

Deirdre answered, "Penelope also called last night. She has made an offer on a house in Hartford. It's closer to the symphony than her current apartment. The third real estate transaction is, of course, this house. But the other two bode well. They say the third time's the charm. Doesn't that mean this will move fast too? Looks like the Lincoln family is going to have a real estate trifecta on its hands."

Emily was appropriately excited for Deirdre but anxious to get the details of the current sale over with.

They were interrupted by the Realtor, who was someone even Deirdre knew. The woman arrived promptly and was smartly dressed, both of which spoke well of her. Without much ado, they toured the house. After only minimal discussion, the Realtor recommended an asking price that was in the ballpark of what they wanted. She also assured them the entire selling business would go well. As far as she could tell, there would be no problems. Somewhat in jest and somewhat seriously, Deirdre expressed the hope that someone would buy it as a Christmas present for a loved one. As someone who had been in the business for a long time, the Realtor said that was not realistic, although she had heard from a colleague it had actually happened once.

The Realtor expressed her thoughts about showing the house. "I hope you leave some furniture in the rooms. Maybe less than now. Definitely fewer knickknacks. I'd really prefer not to need a fluffer. This house has the potential to show well, even though it is currently in a state of flux. Just help me a little on this."

"Is the grand piano staying for now?" The agent sounded eager. "Leaving the piano will show people how big the room is. It would help if the master bedroom were also somewhat intact."

"I would love to have an excuse to leave the piano for the time being." Emily was relieved. "Molly will just have to wait. The delay will give me more time to figure out where it can possibly fit in." It was an obvious problem that Emily had not yet resolved. She added that the piano and all the furniture would be moved right after Thanksgiving. She continued. "The only room that has changed substantially is the library, which looked better three weeks ago, but we're not going to restore it. Nor can we."

The agent was reassuring. "That's okay. A lot of people would be discouraged by the number of books that I imagine were in there. Just look at the number of shelves. It sounds like I don't read, but I know I haven't read that many books. Ever. Most people don't have that many – even display books. I know your father was an avid reader. I can only imagine the number of books that room once held. To prospective buyers, blank shelves are like a blank canvas. People will be left to imagine their own curios on those shelves. Or they can picture how they can decorate. The rooms will be left up to people's imaginations. It's one of the secrets of selling a house. This house should move. I hope I'm not raising your expectations, but I have good feelings about the prospects."

Emily was quick to respond. "Not in the slightest. I think we all have mixed emotions about selling the house. But we don't want a white elephant around our necks. All our lives are tied up in this place. It's tough for all of us."

Emily's words reflected Deirdre's own sentiments. Deirdre was not quite as anxious to have the house sell right away, though. She was loathe to see strangers in her family's house. She picked up where Emily left off. "Uncle David is the executor. He will handle all the details of the sale. He couldn't be here today because he had an important meeting he couldn't get out of, but he'll oversee our end of the sale."

After settling the details, the Realtor was encouraging about the condition of the house and the rooms. "The fact that some of the upstairs bedrooms are used in other ways right now is also good. It shows versatility. Your family life must have been quite something. It shows that there were a lot of changes. I don't think your family was boring."

The Realtor left. Doubtless she had other houses to show and, with any luck, sell. Later that day, the sign went up. The house was on the market. Now the pressure was on to finish the job of emptying the rooms. Deirdre found that it was most useful to work in the obscure parts of the house when viewings were scheduled. On those occasions, if she had advance notice, she would leave the house and take a long walk. If the Realtor indicated that the client was a good prospect when she called to say they were coming to view the house, Deirdre would conveniently go to visit Emily. That way, they could get their expectations raised together. Then, oftentimes, they'd have them dashed together. This happened repeatedly. Deirdre found herself looking forward to those trips to Emily's house. Misery loves company.

The first big onslaught came when other Realtors were invited for their initial viewing. Deirdre was encouraged by the response. Locals seemed to appreciate the house. She even heard one woman say she had waited for years for this particular house to be on the market. The first two weeks saw a lot of curiosity seekers but no buyers. Then a few people who seemed to be interested appeared. Deirdre and Emily were left hanging anytime anyone came to look. Penelope and Caroline heard if the prospect was a truly serious one. Deirdre was sure that anyone selling a house went through exactly the same emotions.

Clearly, the length of time that the family had lived there made it especially hard for either Emily or Deirdre to think about the sale. But, with any luck, the family's tenure in the house would also be an asset toward helping it sell. The whole process was a double-edged sword. All four sisters had strong emotions about the sale. It was their home that was on the market, after all. They were just distressed to see it slip away. However, they were also chomping at the bit to sell the house and have the whole process over with. They could hardly imagine that anyone would not be totally entranced by the property. The family and the Realtor agreed that the house should sell quickly. All in all, it would be nice if the sale were made before Thanksgiving. That way the family would no longer have the burden of an unsold house. It would be a much more festive holiday if they were relieved of the whole business.

HALLOWEEN

CONSISTENCY IS THE HOBGOBLIN OF LITTLE MINDS. DEIRDRE doubted that Mrs. Thatcher, her cherished teacher in high school, had Halloween in mind when she repeatedly recited that old saw. Deirdre thought it was appropriate to this particular day, in this particular house. As a teen, she had considered the subject of her mother's inflexibility many times. Now she found herself mulling over that refusal to change at great length. She tipped her hat to Mrs. Thatcher for providing words for her thoughts.

Looking at those years in retrospect, Deirdre realized that she had much to be angry about. Of all the red-letter days in the calendar, religious holidays, national holidays, three-day weekends and just special occasions, Halloween especially added fuel to her anger. In grade school, friends' mothers had devoted a lot of time to helping their children with their costumes. Claire had never given her daughters that courtesy. As young girls, Deirdre and her sisters had always had to improvise. She had never ceased to resent that. She'd never felt her costume was anything but run-of-the-mill at best. Aside from the candy, costumes were the main reason for trick-or-treating, weren't they? To represent a character or an idea in a well-thought-out and imaginative way – that was the whole point of Halloween, wasn't it? Everybody knew that.

There was that one year their father had spent a lot of time helping the girls make special outfits. That was before the younger girls were old enough to go out. That Halloween, Emily had been dressed as a can of Campbell tomato soup. Deirdre had accompanied her as a Saltine cracker. Derek had been creative both in coming up with the idea and then helping create the costumes. But that had been a rare year. Their father had not always had the time to help them at Halloween. Most years, they were on their own.

The first Halloween Caroline had been old enough to go out had also been the last year that Emily canvassed for treats. Their father had helped them that year too. Once again, he had been struck by the creative genius. Emily was Alice; Deirdre was the Red Queen; and Caroline, gripping her father's hand tightly and stumbling along, was the Cheshire Cat. In the spirit of the occasion, Derek had made himself a sandwich board costume and was the Knave of Hearts. What little candy given him by softhearted people, mostly parents themselves, had been divided between Emily and Deirdre. Caroline didn't know anything about getting candy; didn't need it; and, therefore, never saw her share.

In subsequent years, when both younger girls were old enough to go out, Derek was able to help them at times as well. But that was when Deirdre and Emily were too old to trick-or-treat.

Other holidays brought her sad moments when she glanced backward. Mardi Gras, that other holiday associated with costumes, also made her heart heavy. There were a couple of years that her French class had celebrated by wearing costumes on Fat Tuesday. She had always felt slightly inadequate then too, certainly not ready to hit the streets in New Orleans.

Then there was Easter. Deirdre had one friend whose mother celebrated the holiday each year by making a tree decorated with colored Easter eggs hanging as ornaments. The tree was a better way to celebrate Easter than just eating jellybeans, although jellybeans were certainly hard to beat. Here too their mother had been outdone. Not only had Claire never hung up decorations, she couldn't be bothered to make Easter baskets or even cook a formal Easter dinner with ham and all the fixings. It made Deirdre sad to hear the kids at school brag about their Easter baskets and dinners. Hungry too. The candy those kids brought to school in their lunch boxes and the scrumptious ham sandwiches only underscored what Deirdre had missed.

Although the family celebrated all the holidays with great gusto, the only other one that Deirdre was emotionally attached to was Thanksgiving. It would be more than comforting, and evocative of growing up, that all four sisters would be together this year. Although there would not be any foods from the Lincoln garden this year, the traditions were not far in the past. They had always eaten the last of the tomatoes from the vegetable garden in the backyard at the holiday table. Even though the warm days were behind them, usually far behind, Derek would have wrapped the tomatoes in newspapers, to slowly ripen on the basement stairs. This year, they would uphold the tradition simply by being together. Any tomatoes would come from David's garden.

In the past, Emily and Deirdre had made pies for every holiday and, as it turned out, for every month. Dessert had always been an important part of every meal for the Lincoln family. It was also a signal, more than the calendar, of what holiday they were celebrating, or at least what month it was. If it was cherry pie, it must be February and Washington's Birthday. Lemon meringue pie meant Easter. A rhubarb pie, while not marking a holiday per se, did indicate June and the end of school. That, in and of itself, was a holiday for the Lincoln girls. To Deirdre, rhubarb pie was the tastiest and most significant of all the pies they ate. Rhubarb was the earliest fruit – a harbinger of the season that lay ahead. The rhubarb stalks had a tartness about them. Settling on just the right amount of sugar was tricky. It was critical not to add too much and make it too sweet but enough to prevent everybody's mouths from puckering. The most interesting thing about rhubarb is that its leaves contain a powerful poison – another of those contradictions that nature is so good at throwing our way.

Apple pie meant September. The biggest pie-making effort started when the apples were ripe in the fall. When Caroline and Penelope were old enough, they joined in. After the apples had been picked, Emily and Deirdre spent one entire day making mincemeat. The next day, mincemeat pies would appear and go in the freezer for the upcoming holidays. Aside from preserving the fruit at the right time, that effort cut down on the amount of cooking they had to do on Thanksgiving and Christmas days. Then, once Halloween was past, pumpkin pies would be cooked and put in the freezer for holiday consumption. Autumn was rich with pies.

As in all past Halloweens, this year a basket of candy was ready for the trick-or-treaters. The kids didn't know the family house was being disassembled. There was no need to disappoint eager children, a number of whom had become used to stopping at the Lincoln house on their rounds. Deirdre had spent the entire afternoon carving four pumpkins, one for herself, one for each of her sisters, even though only Emily was in town. Deirdre felt they should all be represented in spirit. She also bought extra pumpkins, enough to make two pumpkin pies and, with any luck, two pumpkin quick breads. This reminiscing was affecting both her stomach and her heart. She could remedy the stomach part. She wasn't sure anything could be done to help with the growing emptiness in her heart, especially as the house became emptier.

The doorbell started ringing at five. It hardly stopped for the next two hours. During one otherwise quiet interval, a little boy, who must have been five, rang the bell. He was trick-or-treating with the supervision of his parents, who remained on the sidewalk. This little fireman wore a backward rain hat and a simple, yellow rain slicker for a jacket. Just seeing him brought a smile to Deirdre's face. *What a charming little boy.* As she opened the door wider, he craned his neck, looked inside with curiosity, and then asked if he could come in for a look. She scarcely knew how to respond, dumbly gesturing for him to come in.

The little boy examined each corner of the room and was drawn to a table with five small, brass elephants on it. After staring at them raptly, he proclaimed, "You have nice toys." With that, he was satisfied and ready to leave. Throughout the whole episode, his parents must have been sweating bricks while they waited for him on the sidewalk. For Deirdre, he was her best ever Halloween treat.

The remainder of the evening passed with predictable surprise and entertainment. The costumes were, for the most part, the standard mix of ghosts, skeletons, witches, and vampires. The occasional offbeat costume diverted her. The number of children pleased her, especially when she discovered that she would not have a lot of candy to be responsible for finishing. The whole evening was a pleasant diversion from working in the house. That would be waiting for her in the morning.

Secrets of the Attic

Thanksgiving was fast approaching. Only a few chores in the house, none of them major, remained. So much of what Deirdre had done had roused vivid memories, most from the long ago past. She felt well rewarded. And tired. The last of the attic and the workshop were all that remained to be emptied.

The attic was the project facing Deirdre when she awakened on that late November morning. If she finished in the attic with enough time left, she had every intention of accomplishing a good portion of what needed to be done in the workshop. It would, doubtless, be chilly in both the attic and basement, since neither had heat. After lingering over breakfast, she started the day's efforts by going to the second floor hallway. There, she gave the chain a determined pull, knowing that this might well be the last time she ever did that. Down came the sliding staircase, and up she went.

Looking around, she was happy to see that she

remembered correctly – no more than ten boxes still needed unpacking. Lunch would be a leisurely reward for a short morning in the attic. She would be relaxed at lunch, knowing that the process of clearing out the attic was completely done, save for dealing with the furniture moved there in the past two years. That would be the job of the movers who would be gathering Penelope's belongings.

Deirdre began by opening the first of the remaining boxes, feeling her spirits sink as she found more of her mother's diaries. Deciding to leave the diaries for later, she closed up that box, only to find more in the next. On top, Deirdre saw an envelope with her name written on it. The handwriting was her father's. Intrigued, she opened it, to find a letter that was much shorter than most of the ones she had received from him over the years.

Hi Sweetie,

The fact that you are reading this means that both your mother and I are probably no longer with you. I wanted you to know some things that always seemed likely to cause more controversy than we were willing to face. It would have brought up ghosts that have been long since laid to rest. But you really need to know more about your origins.

I have always loved you more than you will ever know. Your fire and spirit – your mother called it stubbornness – always endeared you to me more than you could imagine. Your mother never had those qualities. I often wondered where you got yours. There was a time, when Emily was about two, that your mother and I drifted far apart. During that time, you were conceived. You always wondered why you were petite and your sisters are tall. This ought to explain it. You get all your wonderful traits from Kenneth Ritter. During that time, as we waited for your arrival, your mother and I patched it up. I have never ceased to feel that I was given a priceless gift.

So now you know. I hope this doesn't change your opinion of either of us. We both have loved you from the day we knew you were coming. I have no regrets. I hope you're not disappointed. I hope that I can still sign this "Daddy."

Love, Daddy

Deirdre's hand, still holding the letter, fell limply into her lap. The words turned her world upside-down. Having read the letter, she had no inclination to do anything other than go back downstairs. She needed time to contemplate this startling revelation. Maybe her mother's diaries would shed some light on the whole drama. And it must have been quite a drama! All of a sudden, Deirdre had a renewed interest in the diaries. Renewed? That was a totally new way to describe her attitude toward them. She had never had any interest in them. Now she was wildly curious. If she got the cartons with the diaries down to the second floor, she could read them in a more comfortable setting and, perhaps, find out more about the circumstances of the year leading up to her birth.

The implications potentially held strong meaning for all of Derek's daughters, particularly Emily, who had been just a small child at the time that her mother's attentions had been diverted.

Getting the boxes out of the attic was a bit of a struggle, but Deirdre was determined. She had accomplished the juggling act of bringing other cartons down from the attic already that fall. After some effort, she successfully brought everything to the second floor. Then she went straight to the kitchen and brewed a pot of tea. Settling herself at the table, she was grateful that tea has as much caffeine as coffee.

Deirdre decided to call Uncle David. Certainly, he could help clear some of the cobwebs away from her mind and arrange a meeting between Kenneth and herself. She had the sneaking suspicion her uncle was not unaware of the facts that she had just uncovered. David could be of assistance in helping her sort through her emotions, even if only by acting as a sounding board. His guidance would be greatly appreciated. She had to decide how and when she would talk to Emily, Caroline, and Penelope about this traumatic news. First, she had to compose herself.

The ringing phone interrupted her thoughts. She knew it would be Emily. No one else would call, unless it was a wrong number. Immediately she was faced with a decision. Should she inform Emily about this major change to the family structure? Still unsettled by the morning's experience, she removed the phone from its cradle. It was Uncle David. She had a momentary reprieve. He sounded breathless. "Deirdre, it sold. We have an extra thing to give thanks for."

Forgetting the confusion that was clouding her mind, she gave way to her enthusiasm. She wondered why she had not been consulted. "What was the selling price?"

David's voice was filled with relief. "The full price. That's why I did not have to consult you. They don't want to move in until after New Year's, so there is a little bit of leeway. Since you've been clearing the place out, I thought you should be the first to know."

Her response was a mixture of gratitude and delight. "Thank you, thank you for letting me be first. But call Emily." In that moment, Deirdre decided she would open up to Emily. "And when you talk to her, tell her I would love to see her. Tomorrow if possible."

"I'm planning to call her now. She'll be happy to have it off our backs."

Deirdre took a deep breath before starting in on what she knew she had to say. "Uncle David, I just found out something that I believe you know about. It has to do with Mother and Kenneth. Do you know what I'm talking about?"

David's response was slow and measured. "Would you be a little more specific?" They were dancing around each other's words, both aware of what the topic really was. After another short pause, David launched into the subject directly. "I assume you'd like me to ask Kenneth to call you?"

Deirdre confirmed that supposition and told David how much she would appreciate hearing his thoughts in the upcoming days. Deirdre was not quite sure of what else she was ready to say at that point. So the conversation drew to a close with the mention, once again, of phoning Emily.

The advent of Thanksgiving meant the family would be gathering together for the first holiday meal in a number of years. She would then return home, leaving the company of the sisters she had enjoyed so much. Or should she say *half sisters?* There really had been no change in the relationship she had with any of them, but everything now seemed different. She felt she was only a fraudulent Lincoln.

Deirdre resolved that, after she had eaten lunch, she would sit down with the diaries and try to make some sense of this quandary. Rather than having the expected long and relaxed lunch, she settled for a quick sandwich. She then headed back upstairs, curled up in the room that had once been hers and impatiently rummaged through the diaries until she found ones dating from the year prior to her birth. Opening one randomly, she read how Derek had been too caught up in events at work to make it to Emily's birthday party. Then, one missed engagement had led to another and still more. Her mother was not one to put up with being ignored. Busy husband, a growing little girl. It all added up to empty hours. What was that old saying about idle hands and the devil's workshop?

Then, wonder of wonders, a new handsome associate entered Claire's brother's law practice. To make this stranger feel welcome, Miriam had a small soiree for him. Of course, Derek and Claire were invited. It was only natural that the town manager's office be represented. The three hit it off, and dinners, followed by casual evenings, ensued. And so it went. Nothing planned. Nothing that even hinted at indiscretion. Just a series of luncheons, dinners, and tennis games – innocent in their origin but not, obviously, in their conclusion.

It was no wonder that Kenneth had spent so much time with them, especially around the holidays. What an unusual situation they all found themselves in. And what a unique and strange group of people. She found herself feeling sorry, first for her father and then for Kenneth and then for her mother. They were all to be pitied. Yet, they all bore a certain amount of responsibility. The whole situation had not come about quickly; neither could it be understood quickly.

Deirdre thought it ironic that she was reading all this in what had once been the baby room. But the diary entries were all very matter-of-fact – just like so much of her mother's life. *Or, was Mother's life only matter-of-fact after I was born?* Her mother's words of long ago carried little emotion. The room in which she was reading was the first room she had ever had and the room she had moved back to when Penelope was no longer the baby. Now that she thought about it, it was more than ironic that she had two successors in the baby room. There was no doubt that they were Lincolns. She would have to read on to find out how that had come about.

THE WORKSHOP

Only the workshop was still untouched, and that only because what Deirdre had uncovered the day before had kept her from moving her efforts to the basement. The house would soon be ready for its new occupants. Whenever her busy schedule allowed, Emily had helped with much of the housecleaning, but Deirdre had done the bulk of the work – on her own. Deirdre had to remind herself that she had been able to proceed at her own pace, selecting the order of rooms in which to work. It had been her choice to come east and undertake the whole effort in the first place. There was no call for thinking of herself as a martyr.

The workshop seemed an appropriate place for Deirdre to digest the bombshell that had exploded on her the previous day. It was the right room to be in to think about her parents, all three of them. When had her father learned the truth? How had he managed to conceal the facts from her, to bring the marriage back together and keep it there, to even look Claire in the face? How come, of all his four daughters, Deirdre had been the one Derek liked best? She had very little doubt that was true. She had always thought highly of Kenneth. Of all the friends from her parents' generation, he was the closest. But an actual parent? This was going to take a lot of time to get used to. Deirdre had to ask what had been going on, primarily in Claire's mind, but also in the minds of Kenneth and Derek. She was overflowing with questions. What had led her mother to turn to Kenneth? What had brought her back to Derek? Why had Claire and Derek been attracted to each other to begin with? Derek was an intellectual, yet a rugged outdoorsman, as comfortable kayaking in the north country as he was engrossed in a good novel. Claire's idea of an outdoor adventure was an evening at Fenway Park. And Kenneth? He played tennis on a grass court if he had to, but clay courts were more his style. Maybe the tennis court was where Claire and Kenneth had formed their bond. In the course of sorting through old photographs, Deirdre had found a few of her mother in tennis whites. She had not believed it possible that her mother played tennis. But then, anything is possible.

Deirdre found herself reviewing the very different ways their mother had affected their lives. Emily, as the oldest, remembered the Claire who was the grandmother to her children. Emily could also recall the Claire who was the young mother. For Caroline, Claire had been the woman who introduced her to the subtleties of femininity. She was also the person who tried to channel Caroline into fashion and unconsciously, or perhaps consciously, block her from higher pursuits. In her mind, Deirdre also had the growing image of a mother who had stifled the very essence of who Penelope was – the person most likely to disapprove of Penelope's career in music, her partner, and her move to Hartford. For Deirdre, her mother's disapproval had been omnipresent, regardless of the situation. It was Derek who had been the constant in all their lives. Now Deirdre knew Derek had not been her father. Well, he had been in all aspects but one. All of them had managed to turn out to be honest, well-rounded individuals. Did their mother deserve any credit for that?

Her thoughts turned to the role that Derek had played in their upbringing. That role was by no means insubstantial. That was clear just by a brief glance at the woman who each of them was. But now Deirdre had to ask herself if Kenneth had played a role in determining who she was and, if so, what that role was. She guessed it was the old nature-versus-nurture riddle, one to which she could provide whatever answer she wanted.

The substance of the letter she had found in the attic was not information Deirdre could just sit on. She had to share it with her sisters. The question was how soon that should be. She would like to have Kenneth with them for Thanksgiving. She would have preferred more time to reveal the news to each of her sisters, but Thanksgiving was right around the corner. This was not the kind of news that one casually mentions at the dinner table. She had to bring Emily in on the secret right away. And Caroline and Penelope should know shortly thereafter. In terms of timing, she just had to deal with what she was handed.

Maybe Deirdre could practice with Jeremy. She had not yet called him, but she would late that afternoon, after she had more time to think about things. Her thoughts would continue to take shape, both before and during her conversation with Jeremy. No doubt her thoughts would continue to form themselves for months to come.

Having only begun to deal with the cobwebs in her mind, Deirdre shook herself and turned her attention to clearing some cobwebs from the workshop. She tried to put her thoughts on the back burner for the time being. Looking at the tools on the pegboard on the wall, she recalled how, as a little girl, she had spent countless hours in that workshop with her father. Or should she call him Derek? This was all too confusing. She imagined that she had caused a great deal of confusion by her very existence at the time, at least for her mother.

She was not making great headway in her efforts. Theoretically, the workshop was one of the easier rooms to pack up. The task was easy in that the contents were straightforward but difficult in that her mind was, at the very least, elsewhere. Time was getting more precious. She needed to focus on the business at hand and leave the personal considerations for later. She was struck by the tools that confronted her. It was in this room that she had learned to use carpentry tools appropriately – how to drill a hole, how to use a miter box, the importance of using a vise when dealing with a two-by-four. She had forgotten how many tools there were. She hoped nothing had suffered from lack of care and attention since her father's death. But then, she doubted they had been used at all. Being ignored is better than being abused. Most of the workshop contents would go to Tom. Deirdre herself already had all the garden tools and yard equipment she would ever need. Thanks to Jeremy, they had an extensive tool kit for home needs.

She hoped that Tom would give Molly the kind of education in practical things that Derek had given her. Molly would need to be able to handle most house maintenance issues that confronted her when she was living alone. Deirdre needed to remember to tell Tom that. That was the kind of thing a father needed to teach his daughter. What a sexist thing to think! Emily was as well equipped as he to teach Molly. It was a minimum of five years before Molly would have her own place, but it was never too early to start. Even now, when household difficulties arose, Deirdre never felt that she could not handle them. All the Lincolns had been brought up to deal with most common situations. Sometimes, she was even more knowledgeable than Jeremy in how to handle the problem. She was certain this was true, to a certain extent, for all of her sisters. They all could hold their own when it came to the use of tools. Deirdre was certain that she had applied herself more than any of them. Molly deserved the same grounding in the practical matters of how to accomplish things using tools.

It was surprising how each of the four sisters had gone in a different direction. Derek had been able to shepherd each of them with sound advice when it came to a vocation. Deirdre would never have succeeded in anything musical the way Penelope had. At least that was how she felt. She loved classical music, but that was the extent of her musical inclinations. Producing it was an entirely different matter. When she thought of politics, she knew that she could not do what Caroline was doing either. She had absorbed enough to know that her father would not have been ashamed of her in that department either. But politics too was not her bailiwick. As for the life that Emily led, Deirdre had to ask herself, particularly in light of what had come to light yesterday, what her father's views would have been on that. She was amazed at how one simple piece of information had the power to transform the manner in which she looked at so many parts of life.

She turned and, instead of confronting more memories, found herself face-to-face with a fat, black spider. Aside from the shorter days, that was one of the unfortunate downsides of November. All the spiders came inside. This was another area in which all four Lincoln sisters were alike. They were all capable, accomplished women, but none of them could deal with anything that had eight legs.

Further to the right, she found the pile of dust she had been expecting when she'd first entered the workshop. The room was in much better shape than one would expect, certainly better than Deirdre had anticipated. But still, it was not the freshest room. During her time at the house, she had found comfort in the way its atmosphere hadn't changed much over the years. Even though the upstairs had changed a lot, it still smelled like home. But the workshop was taking that familiarity to an extreme. She was more than ready for fresh air. After spending time in the past, she now needed to finish and just pack up the workshop's contents. Into boxes went tools. Nails, screws, and washers were all in separate jars. That made them easier to pack than if they had been loose. Her father had been much tidier than she would ever hope to be. This organization was appreciated now.

Deirdre alternated between packing and thinking. While she was doing the packing, she tried to figure out what she was going to say to Emily, how she would approach the whole subject. Then more tools went into boxes, and more drawers were emptied.

Seeing workshop contents she had not even glimpsed in years, she found herself lost in her childhood. She was a little girl learning how to use a saw. The special techniques learned at Derek's side were ones she used to this day. In her mind, she was still a young girl learning the fundamentals of woodworking when Emily arrived.

Deirdre was a little startled, but she was, after all, the one who had invited the intrusion. After a minimum of chitchat, she tackled the topic head-on. "Emily, I learned the most amazing fact yesterday in the attic. You are my half sister."

Emily looked at her as if she had lost her mind. "What are you talking about?"

Deirdre expected that reaction of disbelief. "Daddy is not my father."

"Of course he is. He always liked you better than any of the rest of us." Emily was betraying herself, showing long-hidden wounded feelings.

"I found out Kenneth is my father. I guess David and Miriam knew all along. Let me turn things around. Remember all those wonderful Christmas presents? Well, you have me to thank. Just so you know."

Emily cocked her head. "This is going to take some

getting used to. I'm sure you've got me beat there."

"Anyway, we both need to talk about this. And I would like to be the one to tell Caroline and Penelope. I can't imagine why this would change anything, but I want to make sure. Weird, huh?"

Emily knew she did not have to reassure her but did so out of love. "It doesn't make a shred of difference. To me anyway. I can't imagine it will to Caroline or Penelope either."

"All those Christmases, all those Sunday dinners – they all make so much more sense. Sort of." Deirdre knew that Kenneth would fit seamlessly into the family. Again, sort of. "I'd like to have him at Thanksgiving dinner. Is that okay with you?" Deirdre didn't really think she needed to ask but knew it would be rude not to.

Emily wanted to help ease the situation. "Let's go out to eat – just the two of us. This needs discussion."

Dinner for Two

GIVEN THE WIDE SELECTION OF RESTAURANTS IN NORTH Linton, with every size, cuisine, and price range imaginable, Emily and Deirdre still chose to go to Morgan's for its quiet comfort and familiarity. They preferred comfort food at a time when the circumstances were anything but comfortable. As they sat down and prepared to order, an awkwardness – one that had never existed before – seemed to separate them. The two sisters had shared so much of their lives. It was hard for either of them to conceive that anything would disturb the understanding that existed between them. They looked at each other plaintively, and their conversation was stilted.

"This is so difficult, Em. I don't know how to start." Deirdre recognized that the differences that had come to light were really only subtle ones. She wasn't even sure what her own emotions really were, let alone Emily's. "This is a new situation for both of us. Being told you're not who you think you are isn't quite something that one absorbs easily. Nor is the fact that your family has been turned upside-down."

Emily seemed as confused as her sister. "Well, it never hurts to remember the things we have in common. I mean, however large a wrinkle it is, it's still just a wrinkle. I am still me; you are still you. We grew up together, and this revelation hasn't done anything to change that fact. We're here mourning the same woman." Emily's eyes brimmed over, letting spill a flood of emotions. "Somehow, this is all about Daddy, not Mother. And he wasn't even your father."

Deirdre felt the verbal slap. "But he was my father." The issue was that their biological fathers were different individuals. They both knew the men that were their fathers. They just hadn't ever known that their fathers were different men and that Kenneth was one of them." Deirdre contradicted her older sister again. "This is exactly about Mother."

It was clear an area of agreement was needed. They acknowledged that they had always felt differently about their mother. Even as little girls, Deirdre and Emily had reacted each in her own way to their mother's mood swings. They had their own interpretations of those responses. Emily thought she had been cooperative and Deirdre headstrong. Deirdre preferred the terms compliant and self- reliant. Regardless of how each described her response, it was plain that Claire had always demanded attention. Derek's distraction had led her to seek happiness in a new place. Emily was only two when Claire decided she would look for fulfillment elsewhere. Claire could never have gotten the attention she needed from a two-year-old.

Deirdre wanted Emily to stop feeling guilty, reminding her older sister that all older siblings go through the same set of emotions when a younger brother or sister is expected. She, herself, probably felt that same way when Caroline was on the way. In this instance, however, it was Derek who was the person being deserted.

Before they moved on to talking about Derek, Deirdre interjected a final question about Claire. "What was the biggest way Mother affected you? What Mother taught me most was about being an optimist. And it's nothing she conscientiously did. It is only in retrospect that I realize that now. It was by example, not by verbal teaching. I don't think her life was a happy one, but she always expected it would improve. And she lived that way. Did she make you feel that way too?"

"Gosh, I never thought of it that way, but I think you are right. What a gift."

The discussion would not have been complete without talking about the man they'd both always thought was their common father. Derek had taken their education quite seriously, both their formal schooling and their exposure to the outside world. He had overseen every aspect of their childhood and teenage education, eventually helping usher them into adulthood. All four of the girls had benefited from his guidance.

As part of introducing Emily and Deirdre to the real world, he would take each of them, one day during each school vacation, to the office with him. When Emily and Deirdre started going to the office, Caroline and Penelope were still quite young. Their turns would come. Emily and Deirdre went on different days to make sure that each had Derek's undivided attention. He did, of course, have work to do, but the day was mainly devoted to them. He had learned the hard way that he did not always have to put his job ahead of personal considerations. Emily talked warmly about seeing her father sitting behind his big desk with the many drawers and then sitting there and pretending it was hers.

A big part of that day was spent teaching them the details of town government and how it was a macrocosm of personal conduct and merely a microcosm of the state and federal versions. First, they learned details about town thoroughfares. Then they became familiar with the town's water system. In both cases, upkeep and finance were closely connected. The girls learned about budgets, only on a bigger scale than most people are normally exposed to. In this way, they were shown that even the most fundamental things have direct financial relationships. That brought the lesson right back to the personal level once again. Claire was not capable, or had no inclination, of imparting this sort of wisdom.

Deirdre parenthetically told Emily about how she had dropped in at the town manager's office earlier that week. Not surprisingly, there had been an almost complete change in personnel. Frank Grady, with his curly red hair now almost all white, was still at the helm of the roads department. The rest of the staff seemed to be entirely new. No longer was she greeted with smiles of recognition lighting up familiar faces. Soon, the family would be entirely forgotten. With their mother's death, Round Hill Road was not likely to get the attention it had always gotten in the past. No more would it be one of the first streets plowed after a heavy snowfall. Nor would its potholes be patched without delay.

Deirdre and Emily continued to speak glowingly of their father's guidance, knowing how he had affected them and aware of the impact he'd had on Caroline and Penelope as the younger Lincoln girls had matured. Lost in the discussion about Derek, Claire was forgotten for the time being. Deirdre allowed that her livelihood was a direct result of his influence, as were those of Caroline and Penelope. As they lingered on Derek's rise in town government, they found themselves gaining an understanding of how his preoccupation with his job had separated him from their mother emotionally.

They switched their recollections to the vacation days they had spent at Solstrand, Ritter, and Lucas, the law practice in which David and Kenneth were principals. Deirdre had always thought that her uncle was the primary instigator behind those visits. Now she knew he was merely a silent partner. Emily had had her own trips to the law office. In that way, she was an equal beneficiary of Kenneth's interest – and, of course, her uncle's.

So the dinner concluded on the same note it had started with – the fact that their fathers were different. Both Emily and Deirdre had received the guidance of one, Derek, and the remote oversight of the other. As had been the case with much of their lives, Claire had been a silent onlooker.

REUNION

The doorbell rang as the clock chimed noon. *Prompt.* Deirdre smiled to herself. *I like that. Nowadays, people pay no attention to the clock.* Kenneth was old-school. He belonged to that generation for whom punctuality was not only important but tantamount. Her father had been a stickler for being on time. Her father? What was she talking about? Her father was on the other side of the front door. But Derek had always been her father. This is too confusing for words. Or for thoughts. She would need some time to sort it all out. Today was just the start. Deirdre was just at the beginning of her fact-finding mission. The facts, or answers she was seeking, started with her reaction to this startling revelation.

The question of her family was blurred in ambiguity – and would be from now on. Well, she considered herself lucky to have more sources to draw from than the average person did. Having three parents gave her more traits to blend together, enhancing her sense of self and underlining her sense of uniqueness.

All of this went through Deirdre's mind in the flash of a few seconds. When the bell rang, she was in the dining room, just a short distance from the front door. On her way to that door, she gave herself an appraising glance in the full-length mirror on the front of the old armoire in the corner. She saw herself blushing. She was acting as if she were on a blind date. Nothing she appeared in would surprise Kenneth. He had seen her dress up in her finest at Emily's wedding and on lots of other occasions. At other times, she was covered in grime in Uncle David's garden. Kenneth had seen her dress in everything in between. She needn't have worn her best clothes for this meeting, but she wore the best she'd brought from home, not ones she was inheriting from her mother. Somehow, she knew that wearing clothes Kenneth had seen on her mother would not be the best idea. It would be in poor taste, at the very least.

Trying to seem calm, she opened the door with a big smile on her face. Kenneth and Deirdre looked at each other without saying anything. Then, as if in slow motion, they stretched out their arms and gave each other a big hug. The gesture seemed both natural and awkward at the same time. Their embrace had the history of their pasts behind them. They had known each other forever. Kenneth was her parents' friend and had joined them for innumerable holidays, meals, and just everyday occasions. He seemed like family. Actually, he was family!

Deirdre's greeting was subdued but natural. "Welcome."

Kenneth responded in kind. "I would not have missed this for the world."

"Kenneth, you look so dapper. Come sit in the living room. It's not what it used to be. I've been busy cleaning, getting the house ready to sell."

"Your uncle tells me it's a done deal. You have to be pleased to have the whole thing off your back."

"We all are." Deirdre wanted to share with him her fatigue. Instead, she just talked about the results of her efforts. "Now that it has sold, I can be more ruthless and can clear the rooms wholesale. I don't have to worry about keeping the appearance of rooms intact anymore. There are still a few comfortable places left to sit. Penelope is going to take most of the furniture, but it's still here right now. I haven't taken away the looks of the place too much yet." They headed into the living room, the room that Kenneth had been in more times than he could count.

They made themselves comfortable, their eyes locking, each of them knowing that they had to begin somewhere, neither knowing exactly where to start. Kenneth opened tentatively, "Well, how about them Dodgers?" They both cracked a smile. It was the perfect icebreaker.

Deirdre thought back to her high school days when she had loathed sports. She joked with Kenneth about how sports were okay as long as you didn't have to do them. Always a diehard Red Sox fan, she had never dreamed of struggling with the stairs in the bleachers at Fenway Park, an effort even her mother had made multiple times. Once the Babe Ruth curse was finally broken, it was all right to let the Red Sox fend for themselves. The hopes of millions of fans had finally been fulfilled, and the team no longer needed moral support. Being a vocal Red Sox fan, though, was a good way to remind northwesterners that she was a New Englander.

Kenneth remarked about her insistence on her individuality. He had a big grin on his face. "I know your mother used to be frustrated by what she called your stubbornness. Derek was proud of you for insisting on being different."

"Oh, Kenneth, you know all my little quirks." This recognition about her desire to be different was more than she expected.

She had many questions about his knowledge of her mother's attitude toward her, more than she and Kenneth could ever hope to address that day. They needed to make a start, though. The biggest question in Deirdre's mind was when Derek had learned that he was not her biological father. Deirdre did not think that he had known it when she was growing up. Kenneth confirmed that fact. He told her that Derek had only learned the truth shortly before he died. Claire, in one of her confessional moments, had revealed the long-held secret to him. It all happened in one of her ever-more-frequent flashes of anger that were common in the months before his death. But Derek had been Deirdre's father for so long that nothing could take that away.

"You two had such a strong bond. He fostered your independence and strong character. I'd like to think that I contributed something there. I always thought the fact that you look nothing like him or any of your sisters was enough of a clue, but that never tipped anyone off. I never could have watched you grow up had the truth been known." Kenneth was pleased at the amount of time he'd been able to spend with her.

Kenneth and Derek had ended up being great friends, professionally as well as socially. They'd developed a friendship that had more to it than the one between Kenneth and Claire ever had. Their intimate relationship had fizzled out. Kenneth spoke with a trace of lingering sadness. "Those months before you were born saw a real strain on the growing romance between your mother and me. Derek always thought you were his, and your mother was anxious to keep that illusion intact. I hope I would have been as good at raising you as he was, but I'm not so sure. He did a damn good job. I'm eternally grateful. You're a pretty good kid, Deirdre."

Kenneth continued as if he had wanted all these things to be known for years. He told Deirdre how his parents had helped him buy his first house in North Linton. He'd moved there not knowing that he would stay but anxious to put down roots. Eager to help David's new associate and make him feel welcome, Miriam and Claire had volunteered to act as interior decorators. The house was a classic fixer-upper, needing attention and much work. Miriam and Claire both spent a lot of time at the house. Obviously, Claire, with lots of time on her hands, put more into the endeavor. Too much. When it became clear that there was a baby on the way, Kenneth and Claire had a big decision to make.

Claire had a vision of the kind of life her children would have. There was no guarantee that Kenneth could provide that kind of life. He was a fledgling lawyer at the time. So he backed away. It was a difficult decision for Kenneth but, even at that stage, not so difficult for Claire.

Claire managed to patch up her marriage. At the same time, she seemed to withdraw into herself. This became much more evident as time passed. The withdrawal was permanent. In later years, Kenneth saw how much Derek, facing this withdrawal, did for all of his daughters by himself. None of them ever suffered.

And so the afternoon went. Deirdre learned that, when he couldn't be with the family in person, Kenneth had gotten updates from her uncle. Then, when the spring rolled around, Kenneth would appear in his work clothes and work with them in the garden. Derek always thought he was a natural gardener. Little did he know. It was only now Deirdre was learning how much of a gardener he was not. Thinking now of the passion for gardening that had turned into her vocation, Deirdre thought, once again, how lucky she was to be in this unique position of having two mentors in the garden. In actuality, it was her uncle who was the second mentor.

Kenneth and Deirdre talked and talked – mostly filling in gaps, not yet breaking new ground. This was a start, the beginning … Deirdre wasn't sure of what. Certainly of many conversations.

Kenneth agreed to join the family at the holiday dinner to come, happily accompanying David and Miriam. He had been at so many family holiday meals that it didn't take much to convince him.

Kenneth left after a few hours. Deirdre felt that the two of them had started a new series of conversations. She knew they had a lifetime of things to say, a lifetime to share both past and future thoughts, observations, and confidences.

Deirdre's head was reeling. This was a day when her past was emerging from the background. Well, at least she hadn't relegated Jeremy to the background. The circumstances of the past few months had taken care of that, temporarily. She and Jeremy had been in communication, talking four or five times a week. She had only once talked to him since the grand discovery. She was relieved and excited that he was arriving in a few hours – relieved that the long separation was coming to an end, excited about the future. She felt as though she had enough to talk to her husband about to make up for all the time they had been apart.

Earlier that morning, Jeremy had caught a flight. The plane would arrive in Boston late in the afternoon. Jeremy would then take a train to North Linton. Deirdre was planning to meet him at the station. Looking at her watch, she was alarmed to see she did not have a lot of time to linger doing other things. In retrospect, she was grateful that she had showered and dressed in respectable clothes that morning. It had been weeks since she had looked that good. Caroline would shudder. There was something to be said for being a recluse, albeit an unintentional one. But Deirdre felt she had accomplished so much during the two months since she'd arrived. Today was really the fitting conclusion to a long process. It was a conclusion she never would have expected but one that left her with much to think about. She felt she had more than earned a day off.

Thanksgiving

THANKSGIVING DAY STARTED VERY EARLY AT EMILY'S house. Emily herself was up and in the kitchen at eight in the morning. There were two turkeys to roast for the fourteen people who would gather for the festivities. If dinner were truly to be served at three, the turkeys needed to go in the oven no later than ten thirty.

True to her promise, Deirdre arrived promptly at eight thirty. Once again, Emily and Deirdre were teaming up to produce a major meal, the last one of Deirdre's visit. They also teamed up to make a seating plan for dinner. It was a challenge at first, but they ended up with an arrangement that looked like it would work. They were confident they had succeeded in seating each person next to someone with a shared interest.

Earlier that week, they had made a trip to the supermarket. This time, the three people who had gone shopping were Emily, Deirdre, and Molly. Upon returning home, they unloaded bags and bags of groceries.

When Derek had been alive, most of the produce for Thanksgiving dinner had come from his garden. No longer. Now, only the apples in the stuffing had come from the Lincoln garden. Fresh potatoes, tomatoes, broccoli, onions, squash, and pumpkin were things of the past – memories, not things to be enjoyed in reality. It had been many years since they had eaten homegrown vegetables at Thanksgiving. In fact, there had been no Lincoln family holiday meal since Derek had died.

This Thanksgiving, people started to gather downstairs for breakfast at random times. Because serious work was happening in the kitchen, the breakfast coffee cakes were waiting in the breakfast nook. People could help themselves on their own timetable.

Caroline and Jonathan were the first to appear. After helping herself to juice and coffee cake, Caroline joined Emily and Deirdre in the food preparation while Jonathan stayed at the table in the breakfast nook, waiting for the next person to appear. He didn't have to wait long before the kids showed up. Tom, freshly showered and looking the proper host, next made his appearance. Then, in quick succession Jeremy, Penelope, and Nora arrived from the other house. Penelope and Nora, in order to cut down on the number of people crowding Emily's kitchen, had brought already peeled and chopped potatoes in jars of water. The only people missing were Aunt Miriam, Uncle David, and Kenneth.

The kitchen had taken on that wonderful holiday smell that most houses have on Thanksgiving. Deirdre had often thought that one didn't really need to eat any of the holiday meal. Just smelling the aromas as the turkey started to cook was enough to make one fat. A lot of the food for the dinner had been prepared in advance. At least as much as they could get away with had. All Emily and Deirdre needed to do with the preprepared food was reheat it. There were innumerable other tasks involved in preparing a dinner of this magnitude. Molly had been pressed into service to help with her first Thanksgiving meal preparation. Her job was to baste the turkeys every twenty minutes and generally watch how the rest of the dishes were prepared. The morning passed with scarcely a free moment.

Meanwhile, the twins were caught up in the Macy's Thanksgiving Day parade. The parade was followed, as it has been since time immemorial, by the daylong succession of football games. Deirdre wondered how they were going to tear people away from the television. Somehow, it had always seemed to work out. Deirdre knew it would this year too.

Right on time at two, the doorbell rang. Miriam, David, and Kenneth arrived, laden with goodies. By popular demand, Miriam had brought the same maple mousse she'd served for the end of that Sunday dinner now so long in the past. So much was on the menu that Emily had not prepared any appetizers. Given the amount they'd all be eating once the turkeys came out of the oven, leaving room in people's stomachs seemed prudent. They would be stuffed enough without wasting space on irrelevant precursors.

Everyone sat down not long after the turkeys came out of the oven. All the food, in the appropriate serving dishes, was arrayed elegantly on the table. Extra leaves had been added to the table to accommodate everyone.

Even so, there was still not enough room. In recognition of Molly's age, space had been made for her to dine with the adults at the big table. Tom dined at the little table with Bonnie and Ben, joined by Caroline's husband, Jon.

The serving dishes made their way around the table. Just before anyone raised a fork, Emily tapped her glass with a knife and waited for silence. "I think it appropriate to mention a few changes to the group around the table this year. We all know that Mother is not here. We all miss her tremendously and probably always will. But we also have two new additions to welcome this year. Nora is a total newcomer. I hope we don't scare her off. And we know Kenneth. He knows us. He's agreed to come anyway. That's a good sign. Welcome to you both. But this food is not going to stay warm forever, so dig in."

Everyone was concentrating on heaping his or her plate with all the traditional goodies. Leery of keeping people from eating but anxious to make his point, Jonathan interrupted by tapping his glass with his knife. "As a relative newcomer myself, I would like to let Nora know that it is a pretty good crew to have hooked up with. You'll get used to the part that isn't good."

Caroline looked at her husband with mock surprise. "We're a bunch of sweethearts. How could you think otherwise?"

The conversation quickly dissolved into comments about the food as everyone became more interested in the main focus of Thanksgiving – the meal. Emily paid a compliment to Jonathan on his selection of wines. "I've never known much about German wines before. I like the tip about maturity. Auslese, huh? I guess I have a lot to learn. I thought I had a decent grounding in French and Italian wines. Now there's a whole new area to be wrong about. Damn."

Penelope rose at a leisurely pace. "Em, I'd like to raise this glass of good German wine to toast you. Thank you so much for having us all. It may be family, but it's a Herculean endeavor nonetheless. And thank you for welcoming Nora so warmly. I told her it was a good family and she thinks I was probably right."

Deirdre was quick to follow on that cue. "I'm happy to recognize Kenneth as an addition to my family."

"Our family," Penelope corrected her sister. Their glances met and locked. Penelope looked at Deirdre with a mischievous grin.

Miriam knew that everyone was dying to begin eating, but she couldn't resist making what she hoped was a final comment. "I'd like to welcome Molly to the table. I hope you will not be disappointed with adulthood. It's not all it's cracked up to be, but I think everyone here will agree that the highs by far outweigh the lows."

Before anyone had time to agree or disagree, Ben was on his feet. "I'd like to welcome Daddy and Uncle Jon to the little table." Everyone laughed, or at least displayed an indulgent smile.

Deirdre saw the proud smile on Tom's face and imagined that if this were not his best Thanksgiving ever, it certainly was the best in many years. She hoped that the presence of Tom and Jon at the little table didn't reflect a permanent rejection of adulthood, but only a temporary one.

Emily and Deirdre had been correct in the way

they'd drawn up the seating plan. No one raised his or her voice, and the conversation was lively. Deirdre was intent on her conversation with Kenneth. Occasionally she tore herself away to spend a few minutes chatting with Nora. Nora otherwise spent her time talking with Miriam, who was very perceptive about engaging Nora in conversation. In those moments when she was not talking with Nora, Miriam was enjoying the dinner without interruption, something that hardly anyone else at the table had a chance to do. David was having a lively debate with Jeremy about peonies; Molly was picking Penelope's brains about musical tempos; Tom, at the little table, was trying to teach the twins about the first Thanksgiving and Plymouth.

As the noise of conversation subsided and the bottoms of the plates became more visible, Emily brought out the port wine. It seemed a fitting end to what had been a thoroughly enjoyable feast.

When everyone had eaten and drunk their fill, the women retired to the living room. Tom had assured Emily that he, Jonathan, and Jeremy would be the cleanup crew. Emily was not going to let him wiggle out of it – not even on the pretext that Jonathan and Jeremy didn't know about the promise.

The shortness of the days at that time of year, combined with the fullness of the stomachs, meant it would be a short evening. They were all talked out anyway. And no one had watched a single football game.

Homeward Bound

It was a foggy, gray-blue morning, not quite light, when Deirdre opened her eyes. She looked around the room, not for the last time this trip but for the last time ever. The pictures that had once adorned the now-barren walls would be hung in her house three thousand miles away. It wouldn't be the same. She would probably sleep in this bed again in Penelope's house, but that wouldn't be the same either. Knowing all that, Deirdre absorbed the shape and dimensions of the room.

Two months had passed since that fateful phone call. Deirdre flew east the day after Emily had called. She had been away from home ever since. It seemed like so much longer than two months. She had enjoyed herself a lot more than expected – a lot more than she felt she had any right to. Emily, Caroline, and Penelope had all made her visit more pleasurable than she thought possible. Deirdre loved being with her sisters.

Emily, in particular, had been great company. Deirdre

was getting to know her older sister once again. Emily had more of Derek's traits than Deirdre had initially realized. She'd inherited not so much his humor but certainly his compassion. Emily cared for more than Deirdre had imagined. People, animals, nature – all concerned Emily more than Deirdre would have guessed. As for her other sisters, Deirdre was surprised at how sophisticated Caroline was and how mature Penelope had become. Despite their differences, they were all remarkably similar. Each had absorbed Derek's values.

Deirdre had grown up as his daughter and had benefited as much as her sisters from that exposure. The biological difference did explain her short stature and her lack of finely chiseled features. It merely put a fine point on the sisters' varied appearances. Kenneth was no slouch in the looks department either. Deirdre was still a handsome woman, just not quite as striking as her sisters.

After a truly enjoyable time with her family, it was time for Deirdre to go home. Deirdre and Jeremy planned to drive west with the furniture and other goods from her mother's house in a rental truck. They hoped they could reach the West Coast in six days. Deirdre had wanted to follow the route that she'd taken when she'd first gone to college so long ago. This time the season was too advanced for that. They had to worry about snow, ice, or even roads made slippery by rain. At this juncture, they would need to follow a more southerly route instead.

Deirdre had been anxious to set out Friday after the delightful holiday meal, but the Friday after Thanksgiving is no time to be on the road. Since it was only a relatively short distance to Hartford, Penelope and Nora had left on Friday anyway, choosing not to spend the entire long weekend in North Linton. They would be back in North Linton midweek because they had engaged a moving company to take all Penelope's furniture to Hartford. The house Penelope had bought was now ready and waiting for its new contents. Deirdre and Jeremy wisely decided to wait, picking up and loading the truck on Monday, spending one more night in North Linton, and setting out on Tuesday.

Caroline did leave on Monday. She and Jon packed up her mother's car with the remaining goods she was taking. Deirdre bade farewell to the posh car she had become quite used to driving. So much was already gone from the house, either to Emily's, tagged for Penelope, or collected in boxes for delivery to the North Linton thrift store. Little needed to be packed into the car for Caroline, since the car itself was the one big thing that remained for her to collect.

At Thanksgiving dinner, each of Deirdre's sisters had promised to make the cross-country trip for another reunion the following year. No one wanted to let so much time lapse until they saw each other again. With the prospect of a reunion in a year, Deirdre was leaving with a lighter heart than she might have.

Tuesday morning was just a repeat of the Friday back in October when they'd first said good-bye to Caroline. This time, the send-off committee consisted only of Tom, Emily, and the kids. Since everyone else had already gone, it was a bit of an anticlimax. Deirdre hadn't actually expected a formal farewell, so she was especially heartened that her departure was not entirely unnoticed.

Since Jeremy had not yet fully recovered from his jet lag, Deirdre was the one who started driving. He fell asleep shortly after they pulled out and didn't wake until they were almost in New York. Once he woke up, Deirdre turned to him with a mischievous smile. "So, we have three thousand miles to figure out where to put everything I'm bringing home. Think we can do it?" After so much isolation every day, she was anxious to resume their regular give-and-take conversations. She let loose with a barrage of questions. The pair had two months of catching up to do. He answered her questions about how the business had been doing and about some of the well-known customers.

The thoughts and plans that had been swirling around in Deirdre's head came bursting out. "When I flew out, I knew I had lost a parent. Little did I know I was going to gain one." The old maple had done its trick, acting as the catalyst for a lot of introspection. While alone in the Lincoln house, Deirdre had learned a lot about Claire, about herself, and about the dynamics of their relationship, or lack thereof.

Deirdre had never experienced a mother for whom affection, let alone love, was a two-way street. It had always been Deirdre's experience that Claire's response to anything that any of her daughters did was certainly not love but, rather, *indifference*. All her reactions were subjective. Love was never part of the equation.

Finding out about Kenneth now caused Deirdre to look at her mother in a different light. "This new piece of Mother's life demands scrutiny – lots of it." Uncovering the hidden parts of her personality and experience was like peeling an onion, only it was a Vidalia onion. Claire was surrounded by a lot of acrid parts, but there was sweetness at the core. The fact that Kenneth and Claire had once been in love meant that the sweet parts of her mother's personality were, at one time, close to the surface.

"I would have thought she would have treated me differently, considering that I was the product of true love, but then there was as much love behind Emily's birth as there was behind mine. It was just that Mother was in love with a different person when she had me. Daddy and Mother hadn't been married a year before they expected Emily and must have still been in love. If only Emily didn't feel that I got more attention from Daddy. Did I ever get the business from her once she learned he wasn't even my biological father! Talk about resentment."

Deirdre lapsed into silence, mulling over her words, as thoughts continued to rearrange themselves in her head. She expressed a simple regret. "I'm sorry Kenneth couldn't be there this morning."

Kenneth had to be in court that day and had been unable to join the send-off party. During the Thanksgiving dinner, Deirdre and Kenneth had conducted an almost uninterrupted conversation. After the meal, he had agreed to visit in the spring.

"We have a ton of things to talk about. Aside from getting to know Kenneth better, I hope he will be able to help me know Mother better. My reaction to her was usually one of anger, alternating with indifference. We know where I learned that, don't we?"

Smiling, Jeremy replied, "Yeah, but where did you get that temper?"

"I don't really know. Neither Daddy nor Mother had much of a temper. I think anger is one of the things that rounds out a personality, don't you?"

"As long as you don't get carried away with it." Jeremy started a longer answer but was interrupted by his wife.

"It's too bad I never got to see any of Mother's sweet side the way Kenneth did." Looking at the road ahead, Deirdre mused to herself, *It was only the acrid parts of her personality that alienated her from so many people. Certainly that's what they did to me.*

ACKNOWLEDGMENTS

This book would never have seen the light of day were it not for Debbie Larson. Because my disability prevents me from using a keyboard, I have had to dictate the book. Debbie entered it into a laptop while sitting next to me. When I lost the ability to speak, Debbie taught me the ASL (American Sign Language) alphabet. It has been a slow process (six years), but aside from ending up with a book, I have ended up with a friendship that means more to me than most of the ones I've had in my life.

I don't know how to thank my loving husband, Malcolm Cumming, enough for the help he has given me, both physical and intangible. He spent countless hours in the editing process, and most importantly, he has given me crucial moral support. Throughout the entire process, from the book's conception to its fruition, he has been uncomplainingly patient.

I also owe many thanks to my caregiver and treasured friend, Toni Jensen, who has done more for me than the usual caregiving. A simple thank-you hardly seems adequate.

I would be remiss if I didn't thank the following

person, whom I have never met. Dr. Jeffrey Halldorson spent fourteen hours in the operating room with Malcolm performing his liver transplant in 2012 at the University of Washington Medical Center. Need I say more?

D.L. May 15, 2015

About the Author

Deborah Livesey, a native New Englander, attended Smith College in Northampton, Massachusetts, the town from which she borrowed Round Hill Road. Deborah was a systems analyst before becoming active in electoral politics. Serving as an Executive Director of the King County Democrats (Seattle, WA), Deborah was selected to be a delegate to the Democratic National Convention in 1988. After the new millennium, she moved with her husband, Malcolm Cumming, to Whidbey Island, Washington. Debilitating Multiple Sclerosis forced Deborah into an early retirement. While losing her ability to type or speak, Deborah used ASL to spell this story, letter-by-letter, to Malcolm and her good friend, Debbie Larsen, who took turns transcribing and editing her tale into the written words of this book. The effort for Deborah to tell her story through the eyes of Deirdre Lincoln took 6 years. Deborah passed away a little over a year after completing this story-telling project, perhaps hastened by the unwelcome installation two weeks later of a President for whom she did not vote.